HOT STUFF

By the light of the fire they both undressed, the flames throwing weird shadows on their bodies. At first she couldn't see him; then suddenly his penis was bathed in the light, large and pulsing. She reached for it and they sank down onto a blanket he had spread for her.

He caressed her, with his hands and with his mouth. When she was fully aroused and ready he slid into her, slowly, until he was all the way in. She wrapped her legs around him so he couldn't get away and then they started moving together, slowly at first and then faster . . . faster . . . and faster.

The last thing she remembered thinking was that her behind was going to be mighty sore from pounding the unyielding ground beneath the blanket.

ANGEL EYES

ANGEL EYES

#8

AVENGING ANGEL

Also by Robert J. Randisi

Angel Eyes

Tracker

Mountain Jack Pike

ANGEL EYES

#8

AVENGING ANGEL

Robert J. Randisi

SPEAKING VOLUMES, LLC
NAPLES, FLORIDA
2013

ANGEL EYES
#8 AVENGING ANGEL

ISBN 978-1-61232-590-3

To Nancy Parent

CHAPTER ONE

Dewey, Colorado

In her comparatively short lifetime Liz Archer had found that bad news travelled fast. It had been only four days since the shooting, and already the news had travelled from Texas to Colorado.

Dewey was a rest stop for Liz and her bay mare, Blossom. She found her town friendly, quiet, peaceful; she also found the men attentive to a beautiful woman. No one in Dewey seemed to know that this beautiful woman had a certain reputation with a gun as "Angel Eyes."

It was all very refreshing, considering the endured hardships that had driven her to pick up the gun, and the things her gun had seen her through since she learned how to use it from Tate Gilmore, himself a gunman of wide reputation.

Maybe things were changing, she thought, as she lounged in a chair in front of her hotel. Maybe the hard times were gone and only good times lay ahead. And maybe pigs could fly...

For the first time in her life—her life since becoming "Angel Eyes," that is—Liz made a concerted effort to avoid the saloon. Men seemed to naturally consider a woman alone in a saloon fair game, and since she was looking to avoid trouble, she contented herself with coffee and an occasional beer at Milly's Cafe, an eatery patronized by the more serious diners in town. Townsfolk who were more concerned with drinking went to the saloon and feasted on sandwiches and hard-boiled eggs.

Liz was in the cafe early that morning having breakfast when she overheard a conversation from the next table, where two men were dining. She deduced that one was a reporter on the town paper, the *Dewey Examiner*, and the other was one of the town's merchants.

"When did you hear about this, Les?" the merchant asked the reporter.

"Late last night. We'll be getting it out in today's morning edition. I worked all night on it."

"It's unbelievable."

"Well, if it could happen to someone like Hickok, it could happen to anyone."

"Yeah, but he was right up there with Hickok, wasn't he? I mean, I heard from some people that he was even faster than Hickok."

"That's something nobody will ever know now that they're both gone."

As she filtered the drift of the conversation, Liz suddenly felt cold. There were only a handful of men

mentionable in the same breath with Wild Bill
Hickok, and she was very friendly with one of them.
She listened further, hoping to hear the name of the
person the two men were discussing.

"How did it happen?" the merchant asked.

"Well, the details are pretty muddled, but from
what I could piece together he was shot in the back
right there on the street."

"Christ, just like Wild Bill."

"That's the way men like that get it, Sam, in the
back, from a coward's bullet. Hell, any man brave
enough to face them ends up dead, so why not? If you
want to make your name famous, sometimes becoming a backshooter is the only way. Ask Jack McCall
about that."

"McCall." The other man made the name sound
like a curse. Then, "When will the first edition be
available?"

"Should be ready just about now," Les said.
"Finish your coffee and we'll get a copy."

Liz didn't finish her coffee, but called the waitress
over, paid her bill, and left for the newspaper office.
She had to find out who the two men had been talking
about and hoped that it wasn't who she was thinking
of.

The newspaper office was pretty hectic, but Liz
managed to catch the attention of an old man who
had ink smudges on his fingertips and on his face. In
fact, he had a huge black smudge right on the top of
his nose.

"Excuse me . . ." she said.

The old man looked at her. He wasn't so old that

he couldn't appreciate a pretty woman, so he set down what he was doing and walked over to her.

"What can I do for you, pretty lady?"

"I'd like to get a copy of your early edition."

"Well, it ain't quite out on the street yet, Ma'am —"

"I know, but I'm very anxious to see it. There might be some news in it about . . . about a friend of mine."

"Well —"

"If you could let me have a copy I'd be very grateful."

The man grinned and said, "If'n I was a younger man I'd ask you how grateful. Here you go, Missy," he said, handing her a newspaper. "Just for you, hot off the presses."

It was indeed "hot" off the presses, still warm to the touch as she unfolded it to the front page and read the bold headline.

Suddenly she felt dizzy; she took a step to steady herself.

"Are you all right, Miss?" the old man asked with concern.

"Uh, no . . ." she replied, "I'm not all right, not at all."

There it was, just as she had feared, searing across the front of the newspaper in bold, black print:

TATE GILMORE SHOT DOWN IN TEXAS,
and below that, in smaller type:
FAMED GUNMAN DIES FROM WOUND.

Her first reaction was panic. What would she do

without Tate? True, in the few years since they met, the little time they had spent together probably added up to less than two months, but now that he was dead she admitted — much too late — that she loved him. He was the only man she had ever loved. Regret followed her panic, regret that they had spent so little time together, that they had allowed their reputations to keep them moving, keep them apart.

"Miss?" The old man touched her arm.

Liz backed out of the newspaper office and hurried to her hotel, clutching the newspaper tightly in her hand. Tears were stinging her eyes and she wanted to get off the street before they flowed.

She started to cry as soon as she shut the door of her room. Throwing herself on the bed like a school-girl, her hands crept into her collar and gently brought out the orange bandana Tate Gilmore had given her — the bandana that had become the trade-mark of "Angel Eyes." She usually kept it hidden inside her collar unless she *wanted* people to know who she was. She cried until her emptiness gave place to anger. Then she looked back to the newspaper, reading the whole account.

The incident had taken place in Winfield, Texas, a South Texas town not far from the Rio Grande. The specifics were very sketchy, but it plainly said that Gilmore — "A notorious gunman of the caliber of Wild Bill Hikcock" — had been shot down in the street from behind by several men. God, she thought, not only had he been shot in the back, but it took more than one man to do it.

She quickly made her decision. It was still early and if she left today she could cover a lot of ground before having to stop. She would take enough supplies so that she wouldn't have to stop very often along the way, between here and Texas. She knew it would take her weeks, and that the incident would be old news by the time she got there.

The newspaper said that the killers had gotten clean away. By the time she reached South Texas the trail would be stone cold, but that didn't matter.

All she knew was that once again Angel Eyes was taking up her gun with vengeance in her heart — and she would not be denied, no matter how long it took!

The killers of Tate Gilmore would pay!

CHAPTER TWO

Liz and Blossom travelled from first light until it was too dark to see. On nights when the moon afforded enough light, they travelled even longer, Liz pausing only when Blossom absolutely demanded rest. She wanted to get to Winfield, Texas, in a hurry, but not at the cost of the big bay mare's life.

Finally, weeks after the incident had filled the newspapers, she arrived.

Leaving Blossom in the hands of the liveryman Liz went directly to the sheriff's office. The door, though, was locked and no amount of pounding seemed to change that. She would have to come back later.

She went to the hotel for a room and a bath, and although she felt cleaner, she was still dog tired. Her reasoning dulled by exhaustion, she was operating on pure instinct.

She went to the saloon and was about to start asking questions when she realized that by making it obvious she was interested in the shooting she might just make people close-mouthed instead of talkative — especially if the escaped backshooters had friends in town. If they did, then the fugitives would be told that she was looking for them, which would make them twice as hard to find.

She controlled her thirst to know and decided to wait until she could talk to the sheriff.

When she tried the sheriff's office again it was still locked. What the hell kind of law did this town have, she wondered angrily, that a man can be gunned down in the street and you can't find the sheriff when you want him?

She returned to her hotel room, determined to wait for an hour before going back to the office, but as soon as she sat down on the bed her eyelids grew very heavy. She fell asleep.

The sheriff of Winfield, Texas, was an easygoing man named Fletcher Masterson — no relation to the famous "Bat" Masterson. Both times that Liz Archer had found his office door locked he had been in bed with a saloon girl, Darlene Leonard. Darlene was a tall, dark-haired girl who was, aside from her huge breasts, very willowy. Fletcher often wondered how her thin frame was able to support her breasts, though when his face was buried in them he rarely worried about that.

Her nipples were as large as cherries, especially

after Fletcher spent a long time chewing on them. Fletcher and Darlene were quite familiar with each other, since they had sex at least three times a week, and their routine scarcely varied. He began by kissing her breasts, licking and sucking her nipples until they seemed impossibly swollen; then he drove himself deep inside her and rode her until she started yelling. Darlene always yelled when she came, which was usually echoed by a loud groan of pleasure from the sheriff as he exploded inside of her.

Sheriff Fletcher Masterson was obviously a man who did not learn from his mistakes — or else he was a man who simply enjoyed sex with Darlene Leonard too much — because he had also been having her at the exact moment Tate Gilmore was being shot down in the street.

When Liz awakened she cursed herself for dozing off and hastily left the room. In the lobby she noticed that she had been asleep for almost three hours.

She hurried to the sheriff's office; this time the door was open. Impulsively, just before entering, she pulled the orange bandana out from her collar and into plain sight. She stormed in without knocking to find a man seated behind a desk. He was in his thirties, with an open, friendly face — a face she might have found attractive under other circumstances.

The man obviously found her attractive — as all men did — for he gaped at her as she approached his desk.

"Sherriff?"

"T-that's right," the man stammered.

Fletcher Masterson had never seen a woman as

beautiful as this blonde angel. Even though he was fresh from bed with Darlene he sprang a huge, pulsing erection and immediately started planning how he could get this woman into bed.

"Sheriff Fletcher Masterson at your service, ma'am," he said, starting to rise.

"Don't bother standing up, Sheriff," Liz said impatiently. "I want to know what happened to Tate Gilmore."

"Gilmore?"

"Yes, Gilmore. I read that he was shot and killed in this town, and I want to know what the hell you were doing when it happened?"

Her vehemence threw him. You would not expect a woman with such a face — the face of an angel — to come into your office making angry demands this way. Fletcher was more accustomed to women coming into his office to offer themselves to him. He was quite a ladies man. Couldn't *this* lady plainly see that?

"Ma'am, ah . . . I don't understand —"

"Tate Gilmore was a friend of mine, Sheriff," she said, cutting him off. "A very good friend of mine. I want the men who killed him, and you're going to help me get them."

"How —"

"By telling me everything you know about what happened — starting with where you were."

"I was . . . busy."

For the first time he noticed the gun on her hip. He'd been so busy looking at her hair, her eyes, her face, her *breasts,* that he'd missed that. Why was a woman like this wearing a gun?

That was when he noticed the bandana.

"Busy doing what?"

He was staring at the bandana; its significance did not escape him. Suddenly, his heart began beating faster, and it had nothing to do with her beauty.

He'd heard the stories of Angel Eyes, of how she and Tate Gilmore were "friends." If this woman found out what he had really been doing when Gilmore was shot . . . he shuddered at the thought.

"My job, Miss," he replied. "Would you mind telling me who you are?"

"My name is Liz Archer," she said. "Like I said, Tate Gilmore and I were friends. What can you tell me about what happened?"

The sheriff shrugged, which infuriated her, but she held her temper in check.

"Apparently, the bank was being robbed and Gilmore tried to stop it. What he didn't see was that the bank robbers had left a man on a rooftop. He shot Gilmore in the back."

"Who were the bank robbers?"

"Some Mexicans. Probably revolutionaries from across the border looking for a little extra money."

"How much did they get?"

"Not much, a couple of thousand."

Tate had died for a couple of thousand dollars.

"Did you catch any of them?"

"Not a one. I was at the other end of town, Miss Archer, and by the time I arrived the excitement was over."

"I see," Liz said, glaring at the man, who shifted in his seat uncomfortably.

"There were witnesses, I suppose?"

"Yes."

"I'd like to speak to them."

"What for?"

"I want to get descriptions of the bank robbers."

"You're going after them?"

"Did you? Did you bother to put together a posse and go after them?"

"By the time I could have gotten a posse together, Miss Archer, they would have been in Mexico — where, may I remind you, I can't go. I have no jurisdiction in Mexico."

"Well, I have," she said. "I have jurisdiction wherever I please."

"Fine," Masterson said, fanning his own temper up a bit, "then you go into Mexico and find them."

"I intend to — and I also intend to find out just where you were when Gilmore was shot."

"That sounds like a threat."

"Take it any way you like. Only you know what you were doing. If you think you should feel threatened, that's up to you."

She turned and started for the door, then stopped and looked back at him.

"By the way, where was Gilmore buried?"

"What?" he asked, looking at her as if she were crazy.

"Where was he buried? I want to . . . pay my respects."

"I don't know what you're talking about, Miss Archer. Why would we have buried Gilmore?"

"You didn't bother to bury him?" she asked, shocked. "What kind of town is this?"

"The kind of town that buries dead people," he retorted, "not live ones."

"Live! What are you talking about? Wasn't Gilmore killed?" she asked, her heart pounding.

"He was shot," Masterson replied, "and I suppose the newspapers around the country jumped to conclusions."

"Then he's alive?"

"Alive and well when he left."

"Left?"

"Yes. He rode out of here just last week against doctor's orders."

"He went after the bank robbers?"

"I suppose, but I doubt he'll catch them."

"Why?"

"The doctor told him not to get on a horse with that wound in his back." Masterson shook his head. "I doubt he got very far before that wound started bleeding again. Oh, he rode out of here alive, all right, but how long he lasted is anyone's guess."

Tate Gilmore knew that he was foolish to leave Winfield so soon after being shot, but he did not want the Mexicans to get too long a start on him.

It had been merest chance that he had been across the street from the bank during the robbery, and that he had seen the Mexicans come out. There were three of them, and a fourth holding the horses.

It had been the fifth one he'd been unaware of, on the roof across from the bank. As he charged across the street to stop them, the fifth one shot him from behind. Once again, his inability to mind his own business had gotten him in trouble — even more serious trouble than usual.

He could recall the pain as the bullet entered his back, high up on the left side. He had been lucky that the bullet missed his heart, and that the doctor had been able to remove it without killing him. The physician had suggested at least two months' rest, but just two weeks later Tate Gilmore mounted his big gelding and rode out of town toward Mexico.

All Gilmore knew — or rather, felt — about the Mexicans was that they were revolutionaries, probably working with Porfirio Diaz to overthrow Juarez. The revolutionaries were in the habit of dashing across the boarder to steal guns, or money to buy guns. He knew he would recognize at least two of the men, but the one he especially wanted was the man who had gunned him from behind.

Gilmore was camped for the night and felt his back stiffening up. He took a bottle of whiskey from his saddlebags and had a few swigs. He felt warm and thought he might even be feverish. The doctor had refused to accept any responsibility once Gimore was astride his horse, and Gilmore had agreed.

He thought about Liz Archer. If he could ever settle down with someone, he figured, it would be with her. What would she do when she heard the news — and she would hear it. When a man of his reputation was shot down — especially from behind — it invariably made the newspapers. When she read it she'd head straight for Texas, he knew, and once she read the note he'd left with the doctor, she'd start after him.

His ride had been slow and painful, and the ground he covered in a week she would probably cover in three days. Still, he couldn't push himself any harder. Already he thought he might be bleeding again. He lay flat on his back, pressing himself against the ground in an attempt to stop the blood flow.

He dozed, dreamed about Liz and awakened with a start. His back was even stiffer. He reached for the bottle and took a healthy pull on it. Just before again falling asleep he was troubled with fear that in the morning he might not be able to get up, saddle his horse, and mount up.

It never occurred to him that by morning he might be dead.

CHAPTER THREE

Liz went to see the doctor who had treated Tate Gilmore's bullet wound. Adam Stone was a man in his fifties, with white hair and a slight paunch.

"How bad was the wound, Doctor?"

"You say you're a friend of his?" the doctor asked, lowering his chin and looking at her over the rim of his eyeglasses.

"More than just a friend."

"I see. Well, the wound was bad enough. He was lucky that the bullet did not strike his heart, and he was lucky that I was able to get it out. I recommended at least two months of rest, but he was up in two weeks."

"He's a stubborn man."

"He's also probably a dead one," he said. "I'm sorry, young lady, but if I'm frightening you I mean to. A wound like that can't help but weaken a man.

He got up on a horse, but I doubt he will be able to travel very quickly. If you can catch up with him, try to convince him to give himself time to heal.''

"I'll be leaving first thing in the morning," she said. "I still have a few people to see here."

"Do you need any more information?"

"None that you can give me, Doctor. I thank you for what you did for Tate Gilmore. Does he owe you any money?"

The man shook his head and said, "All paid up, young lady."

"Good. Thank you, again."

"Please," he said as she started for the door, "I worked much too hard on your friend for him to throw my work away. Find him and sit on him, if you have to."

"I will, Doctor. Don't you worry."

When Liz had confronted the sheriff in his office she had had the urge to go to her room for another good cry, this time from relief. Tate was alive! She realized, however, that that would be a waste of time. What she had to do, she figured, was talk to the doctor, the witnesses to the robbery, and learn as much as she could before she left town in the moring. She was going to try and catch Tate. With his wound, she didn't think he'd be able to travel very quickly — the doctor had verified that.

From the doctor's office she went to the livery to check on Blossom. The liveryman told her the bay mare was in good shape, and would be ready to go in the morning, although he personally recommended more rest for her. Liz agreed, and regretted that she would not be able to give Blossom the rest she deserved.

Later, after buying her travelling supplies, Liz returned to her hotel and sank into a hot bath. She had spoken to four witnesses — two who had been inside the bank, and two others who had seen the shooting outside — and now while she bathed she mulled over what they had told her.

The two inside the bank — a customer and a teller — had told her basically the same thing, except that the teller had said there were three men and the customer insisted there were four. They both agreed the men were Mexican and confirmed that the bandits had not bothered to wear bandanas over their faces. They had pulled out their weapons while one man had shouted in English, demanding all the money. The other men remained silent.

The people who had witnessed the shooting — both townspeople and merchants who were walking past — said that the man who had been shot came running across the street shouting, "Hold it!" before he was shot from behind by a man on a roof. She asked if either of them had seen the man on the roof. One said yes and that he was obviously Mexican.

That didn't help much. Liz already knew that the robbers were Mexicans, and that had made it a pretty safe bet that the man on the roof was Mexican as well.

She turned her thoughts to Tate Gilmore then as she rubbed her legs with soap. While she thought about him her strokes got longer and slower until she was simply running her fingertips over her calves and her thighs. After that she began to soap her breasts, remembering the first time she and Tate had made love, and then the last time. Her nipples swelled as she slid a finger between her thighs, probing . . . and then she snatched her hand away. She got out of the bath, dried herself off quickly, and got dressed.

She went out to find some dinner and ate it, paying no attention to its taste. Liz was impatient to leave but she had to give Blossom time to rest after the hard ride she'd given her coming here.

Over dinner an idea occurred to her. When she left the cafe she went to the sheriff's office, wondering if he would be there. The door was open, but she didn't find the lawman there, just a deputy.

"Sheriff around?"

"No, ma'am," the deputy said, staring at her. Jed Lewis was a young man in his early twenties and he couldn't take his eyes from her face. There were no women in Winfield who looked like *this* — not even at Miss Eva's whorehouse.

"You a friend of his?"

"Not particularly. I was here earlier talking to him about the bank robbery."

"Oh." Jed looked at the gun on her hip and wondered why she was interested in a bank robbery. Could this gorgeous woman be a lawman — uh, law*woman* — or even a bounty hunter?

"Tell me something, Deputy."

Too struck to say anything, Jed settled on just nodding.

"Are there any Mexicans in this town?"

"The only Mexicans we've had lately were the ones who robbed the bank —"

"I don't mean strangers," she said, cutting him off, "I mean do you have any living here?"

"Oh, no, we don't. Why? You figure maybe somebody who lived here set up the bank job?"

"It occurred to me."

"Sorry I can't help you, ma'am. We got no Mexicans living in Winfield."

"Well, thanks anyway."

"Sure."

She started for the door, then thought of something else she should take care of before leaving town.

"Deputy, where's the sheriff?"

"Ma'am?"

"The sheriff. Where is he now? In fact, where is he usually when he's not here?"

The deputy looked embarassed, avoided her eyes and said, "Uh, ma'am . . ."

That could only mean one thing. The sheriff was at the town whorehouse.

"Is that where he was when Tate Gilmore was shot?"

"Ma'am . . ." he said again, looking uncomfortable. "I really couldn't say . . ."

"You don't have to," Liz said as she stormed out the door.

So Masterson was with some whore when Tate was being shot! Well, he was about to learn a much better way of doing his job than that!

Sheriff Masterson was plowing into Darlene Leonard pretty good when the door suddenly burst open.

"What the hell —" he exploded, rolling over. He stopped short when he saw Liz Archer standing in the doorway.

"Who the hell are you?" Darlene Leonard asked.

"Just shut up and mind your own business, miss," Liz said. She stepped into the room and slammed the door behind her.

"Get off the bed," she told Masterson.

"Get off the — I haven't got any pants on!"

"That's all right. I'm prepared to be totally unimpressed. Get off."

"Lady," he blustered, "I'm the law —"

"Wrong," she snapped, cutting him off, "you're a poor excuse for a lawman who happens to be a naked man, at the moment, and nothing more. Get . . . off . . . the . . . bed!"

"This is ridiculous," he said, reaching for his pants, which were hanging on the back of a chair within arm's reach of the bed.

Liz took out her gun, pointed it at him and cocked the hammer.

"Don't make me say it again."

Masterson got his feet tangled in the bedsheets as he was trying to get up, almost fell on his face, then stood next to the bed, holding his hands in front of his genitals.

"Put your hands on your head."

He obeyed. Darlene Leonard was trying to become part of the wall behind the bed, though her huge tits made that task impossible. At least she was being quiet . . .

Liz walked closer to the sheriff and with the barrel of her gun nudged his heavy, hanging balls. His penis, which had still been semi-erect until then, suddenly shriveled up and tried to hide.

"I'm going to shoot it off, Sheriff, unless you answer my questions truthfully. Do you understand?"

"This is very foolish of you, Miss Archer. I'm the law here —"

"Is it understood?" she repeated, jabbing the gun into his testicles.

"Yes," he answered in a high-pitched, frightened voice.

"Is this what you were doing when Tate Gilmore got shot trying to do your job?"

"Well —"

"Is it?" Jab.

"Yes!"

"This is how you do your job, huh?"

No answer.

"Well, I'll tell you what. Tomorrow you're going to hand in your badge so you and miss cow-tits here can spend as much time in bed as you like."

"Hand in my —"

"If you don't, I'll come back and I will shoot it off," she said, and then added, "Although I don't think it would be much of a loss to anyone." She gave his penis a flick with the gun and then backed away.

"I'll . . . I'll arrest you —"

"And have everyone in town know that a woman caught you with your pants down and made a fool of you? Or how about having them find out where you were and what you were doing when their bank was being robbed?"

Masterson's eyes darted about the room nervously.

"And you, sweetheart," Liz said, addressing the whore. "You can do better than this poor excuse for a man — and maybe you will, when he's not sheriff anymore, huh?" She looked at Masterson and said, "Maybe the attraction will be gone then, don't you think?"

The woman looked at Masterson, then at Liz and said, "What attraction?"

"Hey!"

"I'll leave you two to kiss and make up," Liz said.

"Don't forget, Sheriff, tomorrow you resign."

When Liz went back to her hotel the desk clerk called her over.

"Miss Archer, this was left for you."

He handed her a folded piece of paper, a note.

"By who?"

"The doctor. He said to tell you he forgot to give it to you before."

"Thank you."

She took the note to her room and read it. It was from Tate Gilmore.

L I Z ,

BY NOW YOU KNOW I AM NOT DEAD. I KNEW YOU'D COME SO I TOLD THE DOCTOR TO GIVE YOU THIS. I WAS SHOT BY MEXICAN REVOLUTIONARIES WHO WERE WORKING FOR PORFIRIO DIAZ. I WILL BE TRACKING THEM THROUGH MEXICO, BUT I WOULD GUESS THAT THEY WILL BE SOMEWHERE NEAR THE CAPITAL, MEXICO CITY. THAT IS WHERE I SUGGEST YOU GO, AND I WILL MEET YOU THERE. I HOPE THAT I HAVE NOT PRESUMED TOO MUCH.

LOVE, TATE

Love?

Tate Gilmore had never used that word with her before.

Was he suggesting that she ride directly to Mexico City and simply wait for him there? What if he never showed up? She knew she'd keep wondering then if he wasn't lying on the ground someplace where she might have been able to find him. No, the best thing for her to do was to try to track him, and that would take her to Mexico City, anyway. If she didn't encounter him along the way, then she would just meet him there.

She reread the note and laughed at the last line. How could he think he was asking too much of her? The mere fact that he had written the note meant that he knew she'd come.

He knew she loved him, and she knew he loved her.

When this was over, they had a lot to talk about.

The next morning Liz left town and wondered idly if Masterson would indeed turn in his badge, as he had been instructed.

Actually, she really didn't care. She had just wanted to put a scare into him, and she had done that. Maybe he'd think twice next time he wanted a whore — and maybe he'd have to find himself another whore, anyway. The one with the huge tits wouldn't be too impressed with him after last night.

She babied Blossom along for a while until she was sure she was all right, then asked her to run a bit. Before long they had a good, brisk pace going, which they kept up until they reached the border.

By the time she reached the Rio Grande, the town of Winfield, Texas, and its joke of a sheriff were just a fading memory.

CHAPTER FOUR

The first day passed uneventfully, if somewhat uncomfortably. The sun stood high in the sky, beating down unmercifully on her. She tried to ignore her thirst between water holes, when both she and Blossom would drink deep of the stuff. Once she stopped and bathed in the water in order to cool off, though ten minutes after she had dressed and mounted up she was just as hot and sweaty again.

She wondered how a wounded Tate Gilmore was holding up in weather like this.

On the second day she arrived at a small town that consisted of just a few wooden and adobe buildings, but at least it had a cantina and a livery stable.

She tied Blossom outside and went into the cantina for a cold beer. Unfortunately, all they had was warm beer. Since it was wet, she accepted it.

The cantina itself was small, with only four small, wooden tables that were all empty at the moment.

When the bartender, a portly Mexican with a gold front tooth and eyes that roamed all over her, brought the beer she described Tate Gilmore to him and asked if a man like that had been through the town in the past week or two.

"No, Señorita, no one like has been here. Is this your man you seek?"

"He's a friend."

"One should be so lucky as he to have a friend such as you."

She supposed that was a compliment, so she said, "Thank you."

She took her beer to a table and considered the situation. Tate had either not come this way, or he had bypassed the town, preferring to sleep on the trail. That way he could continue to travel in a straight line rather than deviating here and there to spend the night in a town. There was always the temptation to do what she was doing, spending too much time over a glass of beer.

She decided that she too would travel that way, rationing her supplies so that she wouldn't be stopping in any towns unless absolutely necessary.

She was finishing the beer when the bat-wing doors opened and six men walked in. In appearance they looked like bandits dirty from a long, hard ride, unshaven, and well armed. Either bandits, she mused, or revolutionaries.

The bartender seemed to know them and greeted them in rapid-fire Spanish. They crowded up to the small bar and ordered their drinks, and then one by one they turned to study her.

She knew she had to get out of there before one or all of them got any ideas — and then she realized she was too late.

One of the men nudged the man closest to her and muttered something she couldn't hear; then both men began laughing.

"Hey, Chico," the first man said, obviously addressing the bartender, "you have hired a new *puta*, eh? And a gringa?"

"*Caramba*, what a gringa, eh?" his friend said. They laughed and although the other four men laughed with him, none of them made a comment. It was obvious that if trouble was coming, it would come from these two.

"Hey, *chica*, how much you charge, eh?" the first man called out.

"More than you could ever afford."

"You think so, eh?" the man said, walking towards her. "Suppose I tell you that I am a great freedom fighter and I have a lot of money."

"I would say you were dreaming."

The man frowned. "That would sound like you were calling me a liar, *chica*. I would not like that."

"I don't give a good goddamn what you like," Liz said, and then blamed her bad temper on the fact that she was tired and worried about Tate Gilmore. She didn't have time to play games with this moron.

Up to now Liz had been seated so the man was not aware she was armed. Now, as she stood up, the man began to laugh and pointed at her gun.

"Hermanos, the little *puta* is armed. Do you see?" He obviously found this extremely funny, while some of his friends looked dubious.

The other man who had spoken moved alongside his friend and touched his arm. "Hey, Enrico, come and finish your drink —"

Enrico pulled away from the man's touch. "I do not want a drink. I want this *puta* in the back room, with her legs spread. What do you say, *Chica*? One of your American dollars, eh?"

"I'm leaving, Enrico," Liz said, moving away from the table. "I would advise you to stand aside."

"You would advise me to stand aside," the man repeated. "And if I do not?"

"I'll have to move you."

"*Sí?* With the gun?"

"With the gun."

"Well then, move me, little one."

"Enrico —" his friend said.

"Stand away, Pedro. The *puta* is going to move me — with her gun!"

Enrico began to laugh and Liz took a step toward him. The man went for his gun immediately. They were close in the small room and she did not want to kill him, so she shot him through the right shoulder, causing him to drop his gun and clutch his shoulder.

The other five men watched in shock as the first man sank slowly to the floor, blood flowing between his fingers. Clearly, they were undecided about what to do.

"Don't do it," Liz advised them.

The five looked at her, and then at the man who might have been their leader, although Liz doubted it. She felt that perhaps he was the man they followed, but he wasn't their leader by any means.

She toyed with the idea of holstering her gun in a show of bravado, but that might backfire and draw them into making a move. This way was better. They wouldn't make a move against a drawn gun.

"Take your friend and get out," Liz told them, flicking the barrel of her gun in the fallen man's direction.

Slowly, the five men moved to their fallen comrade and hauled him to his feet, causing him to cry out in pain.

"I will not forget you!" the man called out to her. "Better you would have killed me, *puta!*"

As his friends dragged him out the door he spat at Liz, missing. She holstered her gun and looked at the bartender, wondering whose side he was on.

"Señorita," he said, "there is a back way out."

"That's all right," she said, "I'll go out the front."

"Vaya con Dios."

Outside the street was empty except for Blossom. The men had either gone to get help for their injured friend or withdrawn to consider their next move. Liz checked her big bay for injuries, but apparently the men had not taken their anger out on the horse — if they had even realized it was her horse.

She mounted up and rode out of town, tiredly aware that she would have to be looking over her shoulder from now on.

Tate Gilmore jerked awake. He looked around, trying to get his bearings, and discovered that he had dozed off in the saddle.

He tugged on the reins and pulled his horse to a halt. Rubbing his eyes he tried to dispel the mist that seemed to hang there, but he had no luck. He removed his hat and mopped his brow. It was damned hot, and he knew he was running a fever.

He was going to have to find someplace to rest for real. He'd been snatching rest in shade whenever possible, but that obviously was not good-enough. He'd been pushing himself too hard for too long, and since he was relatively near the capital city he felt he could afford about a day's rest to regain his strength before he rode in.

He replaced his hat and urged his horse forward. At the first house or hut he came across he would try to get some help. With a day's rest behind him, he'd be ready for Mexico City.

He hoped.

CHAPTER FIVE

It took them long enough, Liz thought, as she heard the shots behind her.

She stole one look behind her to confirm what she already knew. The five men from the bar, without their wounded friend, were riding after her, firing as they rode. It had taken them a full day to catch up to her, and now she had to push Blossom a hell of a lot harder than she wanted to in order to get away from them.

"All right, girl, let's go," she said, digging her heels into Blossom's sides. That was all it took to set the big bay off. With each stride she gained speed until the ground was flying past under Blossom's hooves.

Liz could still hear the shots behind her, but none came even close, and they were not as loud as they had been before.

The men were persistent, though, and eventually the hard riding that Blossom had gone through of late started to tell on her. She began to labor and slow down. The sounds of the shots told her the men were coming closer, and Liz knew she was going to have to think of something.

Suddenly, just as she was considering stopping and facing the men, shots rang out from a different direction. Liz looked to her right and saw a half dozen men riding to intercept the men who were chasing her, firing at them as they rode. From her vantage point and her hurried look at them, Liz couldn't distinguish anything about this new bunch. Maybe it was just a rival bandit gang who wanted her for themselves.

Well, even if that were the case, she knew she had to ease up on Blossom before the horse dropped, so she reined the bay in and turned to watch the action.

The original five men who had been chasing her had turned tail and were running, pursued by the six newcomers. She dismounted and patted Blossom's nose, talking to her.

"Take deep breaths, girl. You deserve them."

While she was waiting to see if her six rescuers would return she walked Blossom around, helping her cool. Instead of the six men coming back, however, three new riders — all Mexicans — appeared and rode toward her, the man in the center riding just ahead of the other two.

Their leader.

She waited patiently for the three men to reach her, knowing that there was no point in trying to run from them. Besides, there were *only* three.

The leader spoke to her first in Spanish, and when she didn't reply he asked in English, "Are you hurt?"

"No, I'm fine. Were those your men who chased them off?"

"*Sí*, they are my men."

"Well, I guess I owe you some thanks, then." When he didn't reply she said, "I'd like to know who I'm thanking — if that's permissable."

"My name is Valdez, Carlos Valdez."

He offered nothing beyond his name. He didn't claim to be a "freedom fighter" or "bandit" or anything.

When he dismounted she got a good look at him. He was a tall man with broad shoulders and chest, slim hips, and long legs. He wore crossed bandoliers and a pistol in a holster. Another was tucked into his belt. And he was quite good-looking.

"And your name, señorita?"

"Elizabeth Archer."

"What are you doing travelling here alone?"

"I'm on my way to Mexico City."

"That is a long ride, and your horse looks exhausted."

"She is."

The man regarded her for a moment then said, "You will come with me, then."

"Where?"

"To my camp. It is not far. There you and your horse can rest."

He was turning away from her when she said, "I really have to get to Mexico City."

He stopped short and looked at her again, and his eyes fell to the gun on her hip.

"Are you a mercenary?"

"No."

"You are a woman. Why do you wear a gun?"

"To stay alive."

"Do you know how to use it?"

"Yes."

Again the man fell silent, studying her.

"You will get to Mexico City soon enough — but you will not get there at all if you don't give that mare some rest."

Liz looked at Blossom and patted her neck.

"Would you like to sell her?" Valdez asked, suddenly. "She is a fine-looking animal. I will pay a good price and throw in one of my horses."

"I'm sorry, no," Liz said, shaking her head. "I could never sell her."

"I did not think so. Come, you will rest and in the morning be on your way to the capital city."

He turned away again, walked to his horse and stopped before mounting.

"What is the problem?" he asked, seeing that she hadn't moved.

"Perhaps you should try asking, and not telling, Señor Valdez."

The other two men, silent until now, started to laugh until Valdez looked at them.

"Very well," he said, when his men had fallen silent once more, "would you be my guest this evening for dinner, señorita?"

"I would be very happy to," Liz said, and mounted Blossom.

CHAPTER SIX

This time when Tate Gilmore woke up he knew he was flat on his back and not astride his horse. What he didn't know was *where* he was lying. Had he finally dozed and fallen off his horse?

He opened his eyes and lifted his head. The girl standing above him smiled. At least, it looked like it was a smile. He couldn't see her face very well.

"*Buenos dias,*" she said. "How are you feeling this morning?"

"W-where am I?"

"You are in my home," the girl — woman, actually — told him.

"How did I get here?"

"You rode up to my door last night," she said in accented but understandable English, "and fell off your horse. I had to drag you to get you in here."

He looked down at himself. He was in bed, and

from what he could tell he was naked underneath the bedcovers.

"I have seen naked men before, señor," the woman said, as if reading his mind. She smiled and said, "Your body was not a revelation to me."

This time he was sure she was smiling.

He tried to say something, but nothing came out when he opened his mouth. He picked his head up, but it felt so heavy that he had to put it back down again.

Finally, he was able to speak.

"I feel so weak . . ."

"You had a fever most of the night," she said. "It broke this morning."

He frowned and said, "How . . ."

"I had to keep you warm so the fever would break," she explained. "I did that the best way I knew how."

"How?"

"I got into bed with you and held you very close. It was *very* warm that way."

Gilmore looked her up and down and even in his weakened state admired her buxom figure.

"I'll bet."

"Would you like some breakfast?"

"Just some coffee, black."

"I will bring it to you."

He watched her as she walked out of the room to get the coffee. They were, then, in a house of at least two rooms.

He laid his head back down and tried to remember yesterday. He recalled drifting off from time to time in the saddle, and thinking that he needed some rest. The first house, he had said, the first house he reached he was going to ask for help.

Apparently, he hadn't needed to ask, and hadn't been in any condition to do so.

When he thought that he could, he lifted his head again to look for his clothes and his gun. Everything was on a straight-backed chair next to the bed.

"You insisted on it," she said, entering the room.

"What?"

She walked to the bed carrying a cup of coffee and said, "You demanded that I put your gun where you could reach it. Are you — what do you gringos call it — on the run?"

"What makes you ask that?"

"Many of you come to my country when you are being chased."

"I'm not being chased," he said, "I am doing the chasing."

"Here, drink the coffee."

He reached for the cup; a sudden pain shot through his shoulder.

He'd forgotten about his wound!

"That is good," she said.

"What is?" he asked, lying back down, taking care to lean to his right to stay off his wound.

"That you forgot your wound."

"How is it?" he asked her. "I know it was bleeding . . . did it get infected?"

"It would have, but I cleaned it very well," she said. "You did not cry out once, not even when I poured whiskey on it. You are *muy hombre*, señor."

"Gracias . . ."

"I will help you sit up," she said, "and you can drink the coffee. Then I will bring some broth."

She slid her arm behind him, avoiding his wound, and helped him to sit up. Then she piled some pillows behind him to prop him up, and handed him the coffee.

"I'm in your bed," he said.

"Ah, you noticed . . ."

"I'm sorry —"

"Do not be. As I told you, we shared it. It was not an unpleasant experience."

He studied her then and saw that she was older than he might have guessed at first. Pushing thirty, she was very attractive with high cheekbones, very black hair, and a buxom figure. He was sorry that he couldn't remember sharing the bed with her.

He wondered if she had been naked?

"I will get the broth."

"Thank you."

When she left the room he worked on the coffee, which was steaming hot, black and strong. He felt better after drinking it. Just to test himself he reached out with his right hand and touched the butt of his gun, bringing a stinging sensation to his left shoulder. He'd be fine unless he had to reach for it in a hurry. Then he'd probably start bleeding again.

She came in with the broth, a full-bodied woman in a plain blue dress who apparently lived here alone and was not shy about helping a stranger. That brought another question to mind.

"What's your name?"

"Felicity Moreno."

"Felicity —"

She made a face and said, "I know, it is terrible."

"No, it's a fine name."

"I prefer Mike."

"Mike?" he asked. "That's a terrible name for a woman as beautiful as you."

"I like it," she said, defensively, and then added, "thank you."

She took the coffee cup from him and placed the bowl of broth on the bed before him.

"Do not worry about spilling it."

"I won't spill it."

He reached for the spoon and as he lifted it to his mouth his hand began to shake. He spilled its contents onto the bed clothes.

"Shit."

"Let me."

She took the spoon and lifted it to his mouth. It tasted like beef broth, and was quite good. She was apparently a good enough cook that she did not need to ask him how it was.

"It's good," he said anyway, and she took the comment with a short nod.

"It will make you stronger."

He accepted a few more spoonfuls and then said, "I have to get moving."

"You have to regain your strength first. I don't know who you are chasing, but it would do you no good to find them and not have the strength to . . . do whatever it is you want to do to them."

After another spoonful of broth he asked, "Did I tell you my name last night?"

"No."

"Do you want to know?"

"If you want to tell me," she replied, lifting a spoon of broth. "Open."

He opened, swallowed, and said, "Tate Gilmore."

"Tate," she said. "That is a funny name for a good-looking man."

"I like it."

She smiled and gave him the last of the broth.

"There, now you must rest."

She removed the pillows and helped him lie back. Conscious of the wound now he kept his weight to his right side.

"I will be in the next room, if you need me," she told him, but he didn't hear her.

He was asleep.

About that time Liz Archer was having breakfast with Carlos Valdez. His men — some twenty of them — were also having breakfast, but there was enough room between them that she couldn't hear what they were saying. Occasionally, though, some laughter filtered over to her, and she couldn't help but wonder if they were talking about her.

"Do not worry," Valdez said. "It is your blonde hair."

"My hair?"

"Mexican women have dark hair. My men have not often seen hair the color of the sunlight."

She had never heard her hair described in quite that way before.

"Are you rested?"

"Yes," she said, "very rested."

She was surprised to admit it, but she had slept very

well. She had not felt threatened at all in this camp where she was the only woman among twenty-one men. It might have had something to do with the fact that Carlos Valdez had slept close by.

"I have seen to your horse. She is ready to travel, but deserves several more days' rest."

"She'll get it . . . soon."

"That is up to you. More bacon?"

"No, thank you."

"Biscuits?"

"Just coffee."

He poured it for her, then took another biscuit and some bacon for himself.

"You have not asked what we are doing out here?" he said, then.

"I figure it's none of my business whether you're bandits or revolutionaries."

"We are not bandits, I can assure you," he said, but then he did not elaborate. In spite of what she had said she couldn't help wondering if they fought for President Juarez, or for Porfirio Diaz.

"Those men who chased you, they are bandits."

"I guessed that."

She had told him last night why they had chased her, although she had not told him of the shooting. She simply said that she had rejected them, and that apparently they didn't like it very much.

"A strange reason for bandits to chase a woman," Valdez had said, but he had let her explanation stand and didn't press her.

After their breakfast he brought Blossom over, saddled and ready to ride.

"We will be riding toward the city soon," he said. "Would you wait and ride with us?"

"I can't," she said, regretfully. "I have lost enough time already."

"You should not ride alone," Valdez insisted. "Not with those bandits looking for you."

"Do you know who they are?" Liz asked. She was still not convinced that Valdez and *his* men were not bandits themselves.

"I have my suspicions, but I did not get a good look at them. You really should wait and ride with us."

"I'd prefer not to, Señor Valdez —"

"Please, señorita, call me Carlos. We are friends now, no?"

"Yes . . . Carlos."

"Good. Then you will wait a moment while I have my horse saddled."

"Your horse —"

"I will ride with your to Mexico City."

"But your men —"

"They have some business to take care of but they will be along shortly. I assure you, they do not need me to look after them."

"And I do?"

He shrugged and said, "Two riders are better than one, don't you think?"

"Yes," she said, "I do."

"*Bueno.* Give me but a few moments."

While she waited she inspected Blossom, talking to her the whole time. Physically the bay was fine, but Liz knew that she was still tired. She should be ridden easily — if at all — but to do that would get Liz to Mexico City later than she wanted.

"Sorry, girl —" she was saying when Carlos Valdez walked up leading two saddled horses.

"What's this?"

"Your horse would be better off if you did not ride her. I will loan you a horse and a saddle. If at any time you want to go on your own way, you need only switch back to your own horse . . . and go."

She stared at him for a moment, looking for an ulterior motive in his eyes and finding none. That only made her more suspicious.

"Carlos, I don't know what to say. I owe you a great deal, already."

"Simply allow me to help you, senorita —"

"Liz."

"Liz," he said, nodding. "That is all I ask."

"Well," she said, "how can I refuse?"

"You cannot."

As they started off she figured that she was safer with him beside her — where she could see him — than wondering if he was behind her.

CHAPTER SEVEN

They travelled at a slow and steady pace, keeping up a steady stream of conversation. Liz found herself talking quite frankly about her past; and she found Carlos Valdez an extremely good listener.

When Valdez's turn to talk came he did so with such intensity that she believed he was telling the truth.

He'd had a difficult childhood, he told her, losing both parents at an early age and living with an uncle who treated him more as a work tool than a nephew. When he was old enough he ran away and joined the revolutionaries who eventually put Juarez into power.

"Now I am working for Diaz."

"Wait a minute," Liz said. "Didn't you just say your fought to put Juarez into power?"

"Yes."

"And now you are trying to force him out and put Diaz in power?"

"That is right."

"Why?"

"It is very difficult —" Valdez started to say, then stopped and thought a moment before continuing. "Juarez was a great fighter, and a great man, but he is not a good president. He has forgotten the people who put him in power, and now we must get him out before he destroys us."

"And what about Diaz?"

"What about him?"

"When he gets into power will he forget the men who put him there?"

"It is possible."

"And then you will fight to replace him."

He took a moment, then said, "I will fight as many times as I feel I have to for Mexico, until we have a president who does what is best for the people of Mexico — *all* the people of Mexico." He pronounced it *Meh-he-co*.

"It sounds like that could go on for a long time."

"Until the right man is in office. I think that Diaz is the right man."

"For your sake I hope he is."

"No," he said, "not for my sake, but for the sake of all Mexico."

This time when Tate Gilmore awoke he knew exactly where he was. He also knew that the warm, naked body pressed against him was Felicity Moreno.

"Felicity . . ."

"Sí, señor?"

"What are you doing?"

"Keeping you warm."

"But, I don't have a fever."

"Really?" she asked. Her hand snaked down over his naked belly, lower and lower, until her hand encircled him, squeezing him tightly. He swelled in her hand and she began to pump him, gently at first and then with more vigor.

"Felicity . . ."

"Mike," she said, correcting him.

"Mike . . ."

"Yes?"

"I'm . . . getting a fever."

"Yes," she said, "I can feel you getting very hot. You need a compress . . . a hot compress."

She slid down until she was totally beneath the sheet, and he felt her mouth trailing down over his belly, taking the same trail her hand had blazed only moments before. Suddenly, he felt her tongue on him, licking him up and down like a stick of licorice, and then her mouth engulfed him, and he *did* have a fever — a searing, *demanding* fever . . .

It came as a surprise to Liz, but then, she had found in the past that many of the most satisfying experiences she'd had with men had come as surprises.

One moment she and Carlos Valdez were staring at each other across the fire, and the next thing she knew he was beside her. He kissed her gently on the mouth, then pulled back, and then *she* kissed *him* on the mouth and pulled back. The next kiss was initiated by both of them. His tongue was in her mouth, and his hands were beneath her shirt, stroking her breasts until her nipples were hard and sensitive.

As she later recalled it, her shirt was suddenly gone and his mouth was on her breasts as she cupped his head in her hands. She remembered moaning and wrapping her fingers in his hair so she could pull his face up to hers. While they kissed her hands went to his belt, but the bandoliers were in the way.

By the light of the fire they both undressed, the flames throwing weird shadows on their bodies. At first she couldn't see him; then suddenly his penis was bathed in the light, large and pulsing. She reached for it and they sank down onto a blanket he had spread for her.

He caressed her, with his hands and with his mouth. When she was fully aroused and ready he slid into her, slowly, until he was all the way in. She wrapped her legs around him so he couldn't get away and then they started moving together, slowly at first and then faster . . . and faster . . . and faster. . . .

The last thing she remembered thinking was that her behind was going to be mighty sore from pounding the unyeilding ground beneath the blanket.

"Do you feel guilty?" Carlos Valdez asked the next morning.

Liz smiled and said, "No," shaking her head.

"Perhaps there is a special man?"

"There *is* a special man, but I do not feel any guilt, Carlos."

"I am glad."

She smiled and said, "So am I."

As the sun streamed in through the window, Felicity

"Mike" Moreno dressed as Tate Gilmore watched. A sense of regret struck him as her perfect breasts disappeared into her dress. He regretted also that his wound had kept him from enjoying her fully — but she had done whatever she could to help him. She had sat astride him, riding him easily, so as not to jar his wound, and at one point she had slid all the way up past his chest so that she could sit astride his face, enabling him to taste her.

She too felt regret, because he had satisfied her more than any man she had ever had, even though he was wounded and could not participate fully. And because she knew that he would not stay around after he was fully healed. Still, he would be with her at least one more day.

She would do what she could to assure that much.

"Where are you going?" he asked.

"To get your breakfast," she said. "A big breakfast. You deserve it."

By god, he thought, and I have an appetite for it.

In Mexico City, in the presidential palace, Presidente Juarez was speaking to one of his advisors.

"Tell me what is happening, Eduardo."

"The revolutionaries are moving into the city, My Presidente."

"I know that, Eduardo. Do we know where they are and who they are?"

"Yes. We can crush them at any time."

"We do not want to crush them," Juarez said very patiently. "These are the people who fought to put me in this office."

"And are fighting to remove you."

"Still, to crush them, would not endear us with the people of Mexico. We need outside help."

"It is coming, My Presidente."

"*Who* is coming, Eduardo?"

"Two gringo gunfighters."

"Gringos!" Juarez spat, as if the word itself were distasteful. Then the president of Mexico leaned forward and asked curiously, "Who? Is it the wild one — what is his name? Hiccup?"

"Hickok," Eduardo said, "you are thinking of Wild Bill Hickok. No, Excellency, he is dead."

"A shame. Who then?"

"There is a man named Tate Gilmore who is on his way here, but his progress had been slowed by the fact that he is wounded."

"Who wounded him?"

"Revolutionaries who were robbing a bank in Texas. This man tried to stop them and was shot in the back."

"He lived?"

Eduardo Soto nodded and said, "And he is on his way here."

"I have heard of him. He is said to be very fast. Will he help us?"

Soto shrugged. "He is after the men who shot him. It is the same thing."·

"And the other one?"

"An American woman named Elizabeth Archer."

"A woman? Who is she? I do not know that name."

"Perhaps you will recognize the other name she used, that of 'Angel Eyes'."

Juarez's eyes widened as he said, "*That* name I have heard. Will she help?"

"She will help Gilmore. They are . . . friends."

"Ah," Juarez said, grinning lecherously, "I understand. He is after the men who shot him, she will come to help him, and they will both help us, as well."

"Yes, Excellency."

"It is an excellent plan, Eduardo," Juarez said, reaching for a huge cigar.

"Thank you, Exc —"

Lighting his cigar Juarez interrupted, "I am glad I thought of it."

CHAPTER EIGHT

"What's wrong?" Liz asked Carlos Valdez.

Valdez had suddenly reined his horse in and Liz had continued a few yards before she realized it and also stopped, trotting Blossom back to where Valdez was.

"I don't know," Valdez said.

"What do you —"

He held up his hand for silence, and she granted it to him. It was his country, and maybe he knew something that she didn't.

"I feel . . . something . . ." he said, staring beyond her.

"What?"

"I don't know, Liz," he said. "It is an instinct that I seem to have. I don't know what it is, but there is danger just ahead."

"What do you suggest we do?"

He looked around and spotted a copse of trees off to one side.

"Let's take refuge there in those trees and wait and see what happens."

"All right, Carlos," she said, going along with him until such time as his instinct proved incorrect.

They rode to the trees, then walked the horses between them so that they were completely out of sight.

"Now what?"

"Now we wait."

"How long?"

"As long as it takes."

She wanted to argue, but decided against it. Instead, she would play his game, though watching him closely. Having had sex with him the night before by no means made him above her suspicion. There was still a chance he was just trying to slow down their — her — progress.

After three or four minutes her patience began to wane, and then suddenly they were there.

"Who are they?"

"Juaristas."

Juarez's private army.

About a dozen of them were riding two by two. Liz and Carlos breathed quietly as the Jaristas rode by, their sabers clanking.

Liz waited for Carlos to speak first.

"They are gone."

"Who were they looking for?"

"Revolutionaries, bandits, anyone they could find. They would torture them and kill them and say that they were being patriotic." He paused a moment and then said, "Come, we had better get underway before they come back and decide that it would be patriotic to kill us."

They led their horses out of the trees, mounted up, and started off at a walk.

"Sound travels easily out here," he warned her. "We will move slowly until we have put enough distance between them and us."

After they had ridden a couple of miles in silence, Liz asked, "You heard them didn't you?"

"No, not heard," he said, shaking his head. "I smelled them, sensed them, but I did not hear them."

"Instinct."

"It has kept many men alive."

"And a woman or two, as well."

Valdez looked at Liz and said, "I suspect you would know about that first hand."

"It's come in handy once or twice."

"And what about now?"

She frowned and said, "What about now?"

"What does your instinct tell you about me?"

She regarded him silently for a few moments, and then decided to be truthful.

"My instincts tell me not to trust you."

He raised his eyebrows in surprise and said, "Even after last night?"

"Especially after last night."

Valdez reined in his horse and turned slightly in his saddle, looking behind him.

"I think we can move faster now. We're out of

their range of hearing.'' He straightened himself forward in his saddle again and said to her, ''Well, you are very honest about your feelings.''

''It's the only way I know how to be, Carlos. I'm sorry if I offended —''

''You did not offend me at all,'' Valdez said. ''I am honored that you regard me highly enough to be that honest with me.''

Liz stared at him to see if he was kidding, and decided that he was not. Carlos Valdez was convincing her that Spanish men could find good in any kind of bad if they tried hard enough.

''It will be dark soon,'' Valdez said. ''We will go on a little further and then we will camp.''

About a mile behind Valdez and Liz, on a ridge, Valdez's men paused in their task of following their leader's trail.

''This is not fair,'' Paco Mendez said. ''They are travelling too slowly.''

''Would you travel quickly with a beautiful woman?'' another man asked. ''Carlos is probably stopping every hour to keep the señorita happy.''

Most of the other men laughed, but not Arturo Fuentes, who was Carlos Valdez's second-in-command.

''That is enough,'' he said aloud. ''We do not question our orders.''

''Orders,'' Paco Mendez spat out. ''Are we Juaristas, waiting for orders for El Presidente to piss?''

The absent leader Carlos Valdez would have silenced the defiant Mendez with a look, but Valdez — who was more powerful with words than many men were with their fists — was not there, and second-in-command Fuentes had to keep the men under control.

Fuentes shifed slightly in his saddle and saw that Mendez was within easy arm's reach. He swung his right hand in a vicious backward arc. Fuentes was a huge, muscular man and his knuckles exploded on Mendez's cheek, splitting the skin and knocking him from the saddle.

"Does anyone else have something to say?"

The other men simply exchanged glances and maintained silence.

"Get Mendez back on his horse and we will continue."

"Somebody is coming," Juan Espino called out.

"Who?" Fuentes asked.

Espino, a few yards ahead of the rest of the men, at the crest of the ridge, called back, "Juaristas."

"How many?"

Espino took a moment, then said, "Twelve."

"We outnumber them!" someone else said. "We can wipe them out."

The other men took up the bellicose attitude until Fuentes turned in his saddle . and commanded, "Silence! To engage the enemy would mean a lot of shooting. Where there are twelve Juaristas there are more. If they hear the shooting they will come."

"They're getting closer," Espino said.

Fuentes walked his horse up alongside Espino's.

"Can they see us up here?"

"If they look," Espino said. "There are too many of us to avoid discovery."

"But they have to look up here to see us."

"Yes."

"Go back and tell the men I want them to remain still and quiet. The first man who makes a sound I will kill personally."

"I will tell them."

With bated breath, Arturo Fuentes watched the Juaristas ride by down below, his hand on his side-arm. Much as *he* would have wanted them dead, it was better to let them pass.

There was too much to be gained in Mexico City to risk it on twelve men.

CHAPTER NINE

Later that evening Liz and Carlos made camp and Liz prepared their dinner. They sat on opposite sides of the fire, eating in silence, until Liz finally had to ask the question that had been on her mind.

"Carlos, what do you want from me?"

"You do not believe that perhaps I only came with you hoping that what happened last night would happen?" he asked, studying her.

"No." Her reply came quickly, and without hestitation.

"Well . . ." he prompted her.

"I'll tell you what I do believe, though."

"What is that?"

"I do believe that you want *something* from me. And before we ride together any further, I'd like you to tell me just what it is."

"Perhaps I hope to enlist you into our cause."

"I hope that's not it."

"Why not?"

"Because I would have to turn you down."

"Turn me down?" Valdez repeated, not understanding the phrase.

"Refuse," she explained.

"Why?"

Liz shrugged.

"I have my own causes."

"As great as the cause of Mexico?"

"This is your country, Carlos," she said, "and it's your cause. We all have our own causes."

"This other man, he is your cause?"

"Right now, yes."

"We could pay you. Of course, you would have to wait for us to win before we could actually pay you."

"Out of the treasury?" she asked.

"Yes."

"Why would you pay me?" she asked. "Is it because you know who I am?"

He shrugged, then smiled guiltily, caught.

"I did recognize your name, yes," he confessed. "Even here in Mexico we have heard of the very beautiful lady gunfighter, Angel Eyes. I thought that perhaps I could get you to come to our side and help us."

"How much more could one person add?"

Even as she asked, she recalled something Tate Gilmore had told her when they first met — one good man with a gun is worth six bad men without guns.

Tate had told her to remember that, and she did; but with Valdez she would probably be pitted against more then just six men at a time.

"A person such as you could add much," Valdez promised her.

"I'm sorry, Carlos."

"So am I."

After dinner, by mutual silent agreement they kept to their own bedrolls, on either side of the fire.

Instinct.

Once the Juaristas passed Carlos Valdez's men, Arturo Fuentes took the men a little further, and then made camp for the night. He assigned two men to watches, and they were relieved every two hours.

Reclining on his bedroll, with his head propped up on his pillow, he pondered if what Mendez had said was true.

Was Valdez enjoying the blonde woman's favors?

If he was, Arturo Fuentes wanted his chance as well.

Felicity sat astride Tate Gilmore and leaned forward so that he could close his mouth on her luscious breasts. He suckled her nipples and she begged him to suck them harder; as her passion deepened she lost her English and began to croon to him in Spanish. He didn't know what she was saying, but the sound of it excited him.

He was buried deep inside of her. With her inner, womanly muscles she began to massage him, squeezing him, pulling at him like a wet hand until he went off inside of her like a geyser . . .

"I'll be leaving in the morning," he told her sometime later.

"I know," she said. "Are you . . . well?"

"Well enough to ride, thanks to the very good care you've taken of me."

"Hmm," she said, burying her face in his chest, "you will make me wish I had not taken such good care of you."

"Felicity —"

"Mike."

"I can't call you Mike," he complained. "I don't think I could ever get used to calling you that."

She reached down and took firm hold of his semi-erect penis.

"Then I will continue to hold onto you until you say you can."

"But what's the matter with Felicity as a name? It's beautiful."

"It is a little girl's name, and I am not a little girl."

He cupped one of her big breasts in his hand, feeling the nipple respond immediately, and said, "No, you definitely are not a little girl, but I think I'm going to keep calling you Felicity."

She tightened her hold on his penis, then reluctantly released it.

"All right," she said, "but you are the only one I will permit to do that."

Sure, Gilmore thought, until the right man comes along.

The following morning Liz and Valdez broke camp in silence. She was sorry if she had offended him, but she wasn't prepared to forget about Tate's life in order to fight Juarez.

Besides, it was revolutionaries who had shot him, and for all she knew they might have been Carlos Valdez's own men.

Tate Gilmore mounted his horse, a small sack of supplies that Felicity had given him tied to his saddle behind him. His back was stiff and he knew he was going to have to rest more often than he liked, but Felicity Moreno had done a good job of doctoring, and he felt that within three days he could be in Mexico City. Once he was there, he figured, the revolutionaries who had robbed the bank and shot him would seek him. Just like he wanted.

He waved to Felicity as she stood on her porch and he wondered — strangely enough, for the first time — what a woman like her was doing living out there all alone.

He had never bothered to ask her.

Arturo Fuentes roused his men and got them mounted. By now Carlos and the woman would be underway, and his orders were to not lag too far behind.

He wondered what Carlos had in mind for the woman if she decided not to join them.

To kill her would be a terrible waste. She was the loveliest woman Arturo Fuentes had ever seen, and when he thought of her he always grew aroused — more aroused than even his own fiery, Mexican wife could make him.

Then again, if Valdez decided that he wanted her killed Fuentes could always volunteer for the job — and take his time doing it.

In Mexico City Eduardo Soto, President Juarez's advisor, lay in his bed beside a sleeping young woman and went over his plan in his mind. He found it foolproof. Once it was carried out, Juarez would be dead and he, Eduardo Soto, would be El Presidente.

During the revolution Juarez and Soto had fought side by side, while Juarez had promised Soto much — now in office, he had delivered very little of it. Juarez had promised Soto power of his own, but in truth Eduardo Soto was now nothing but a servant to Juarez. Why, Juarez had not even named him Vice-President. Yes, Soto had been given a big office, and a. fancy apartment, and his pick of the women of Mexico City — like the busty, thick-thighed, black-haired cantina girl in bed next to him right now — but that wasn't enough for a man of Eduardo Soto's amibitions.

He wanted more.

And soon — very soon, he promised himself — he would have it.

Meanwhile, he slapped the girl on the ass hard, jerking her awake. He might as well enjoy what little he had while he was waiting.

"Come, on your knees!"' he commanded. *"Vamanos!"*

"This is silly," Carlos Valdez finally said.

"What is?" Liz asked.

They had ridden most of the day in silence.

"Not speaking to each other," the man said. "I truly do not want to hold your decision against you, Liz. It's just that I think you could be of great help to us."

"I don't see how."

"If I could think of a way, and you were . . . available, would you think about it?"

There was no harm in agreeing to that.

"Sure, Carlos, I'd think about it."

"Bueno," Valdez said. "That is all I ask of you now."

"All right."

"This friend of yours," Carlos said, "this man, does he know how lucky he is?"

"I'm not sure he does," Liz responded, "but I intend to tell him."

The disjointed procession continued on to Mexico City: Tate Gilmore rode in the lead, though now only by a few days. Behind him came Liz Archer and Carlos Valdez, and behind them Valdez's men, led by Arturo Fuentes. Fuentes and the band had made one stop to pick up another of their number, but that had not slowed them down.

Waiting for them in the capital city was El Presidente Juarez, his Juaristas, and his supposed loyal aide, Eduardo Soto.

When all groups arrived — and converged — Mexico City would be like a powder keg with many fuses, all burning furiously.

There would be a big bang — but bigger for some than for others.

CHAPTER TEN

Father John Miguel de la Vega knelt before the statue of the Holy Mother and prayed. He prayed for the preservation of Mexico, Mexico City, and the Mexican people. He knew what was coming and he prayed that all would go well, that a minimum of his flock would die. The Church of the Sacred Heart — one of the smaller churches in the city — did not have that many parishioners to begin with.

The priest rose and left the church, walking into his office. He walked to a large cedar chest against one wall, knelt before it and opened it. He removed everything until he found what he wanted, at the bottom, carefully wrapped to keep it clean. He removed it, replaced everything else in the chest, then walked to his desk and unwrapped his prize.

A Deane-Adams revolver rested in a smooth leather holster. He took out the gun, checked it carefully, then replaced it in the holster. He raised his robes and strapped the gun on. He would oil it soon, but he wanted to see how it felt back on his hip after all this time.

To his shame he experienced a thrill as he felt the familiar weight of the gun on his hip. He lowered his robe, then raised it quickly and drew the gun. Hastily he shed the robes, then reached for the gun again. Smooth — some things you never forget — but slow, slower than ever before. It would take work, but he felt that he was not far from top form with the gun.

Of course, he had no intentions of using the weapon — that is, unless he happened to come face to face with El Presidente, Juarez, himself.

In which case he would blow the *cabrone's* fucking head off.

Juarez sat in his office in the presidential palace with his feet on the desk and thought how ungrateful these peasants were. He had given them back their country and look how they repaid him. Death threats, assassination attempts.

Jesus Cristo, now that the foolish people had a real leader they did not know what to do with him!

Tate Gilmore finally arrived in Mexico City but it gave him no great sense of accomplishment. It had taken him so long to get there that the bandits might have already staged a successful revolution. Hell, the man he was looking for might well be president by now.

Of the many hotels in Mexico City Gilmore deliberately chose one far away from the presidential palace. If anyone was really serious about dethroning Presidente Juarez, he figured, they might choose to do it by blowing up the palace. Staying in a hotel too near the palace might be very dangerous.

He put up his horse at a livery stable and returned to his room to rest. Although his back was still stiff, he felt surprisingly well for a man in his condition.

So well, in fact, that he fell asleep almost as soon as he hit the bed — without meaning to.

Two days outside of Mexico City Liz and Valdez paused to rest their horses. Liz was now riding relatively rested Blossom again and Valdez was leading the extra horse.

"What will you do when we reach the city?" Liz asked.

"Get in touch with some of my people. We are very close —" he started to say, then stopped short.

"Very close to what?"

He looked at her and said, "Very close to a solution, but I cannot tell you much more than that, unless . . ."

"Unless I agree to help you."

"Yes."

"Which I can't do, yet."

"Perhaps, when we get into the city we will be able to change your mind."

"We?"

"I will arrange for you to meet some of the others. Perhaps, after you speak with them . . ."

"I have to resolve my problem before I do anything."

"You mean your . . . your friend's problem."

In spite of the fact that they had not slept together since that first time she thought she detected a hint of jealousy in his tone.

"Yes, my friend's problem."

Valdez patted his horse's neck. "I might have a solution to that."

"Like what?"

"What if we helped you with your problem . . . and your friend's problem . . . would you be willing to help us with ours, in return?"

Liz considered the question. If anyone could help her and Tate find out who had shot him, it might very well be Carlos Valdez.

"I think I could agree to that, Carlos — if my friend will."

"Your friend? Why should he have to agree? We will help him with his problem and then he can be on his way and you can help us with ours."

"Look, you're trying to . . . to save a whole country, Carlos. I don't know how I can help you with that, but if you insist on using me in some way, I'm sure you could use my friend, as well."

"Why? Who is he?"

"His name is Tate Gilmore."

"Tate . . ." he said.

It was obvious that he recognized the name.

"Tate Gilmore."

"That's right."

"The . . . the gunman."

"He has a certain reputation."

Valdez patted his horse's neck again, staring straight ahead.

"So?" Liz said.

"We should get started. If we ride at night we can be in Mexico City by late tomorrow."

"Riding at night is dangerous."

"Not if you know where you are going," he replied, "and I do."

"What about Tate —"

"We can talk about it when we get to the city."

"Why not now?"

"Because —" he started, and was cut off by the sound of shots.

"Juaristas!" he shouted. "Let's ride!"

He spurred his horse on, dropping the reins of the second horse, and she followed. Behind them a platoon of Juaristas rode hard after them, firing even though they were too far away.

Liz felt sure that she and Carlos could outrun the Juaristas, because the two had a good head start on them. Once safely away, she would broach the subject of Tate Gilmore again.

Tate's name had obviously affected Carlos Valdez, and she had a feeling that perhaps she was closer to finding out who had shot Tate than she thought.

"Shots," Arturo Fuentes said.

"Carlos?" Mendez said.

"Possibly."

"Juaristas, then. We have to help him."

"We cannot."

"Why?"

Fuentes looked at Mendez and said, "We are too far away, and Carlos told us not to show ourselves to the woman."

They could still hear the shots when Juan Espino came riding back to them.

"Juan?" Fuentes prompted.

"Juaristas, a platoon. They are chasing Carlos and the woman."

"Are they in immediate danger?"

Espino made a face.

"The fools, they started firing before they were in range. They are chasing them, but I do not think they will catch them."

Too bad, Fuentes thought. He'd had visions of taking Carlos' place in the revolution, and if the Juaristas had caught and killed the man, it would have made it so much easier.

"We'd better get moving while the Juaristas are busy with them," the woman on Fuentes' right said. "Our people will be waiting in Mexico City."

"All right, Felicity."

Felicity Moreno glared at the Mexican. "Don't call me Felicity!"

CHAPTER ELEVEN

Late the next evening Liz and Carlos Valdez rode into Mexico City. They had ridden most of the night, pausing only from time to time to rest the horses. Neither one of them voiced it, but they both knew they could have used that lost extra horse. Still, unencumbered with it they had been able to successfully outrun the Juaristas.

Just before entering the city they stopped to talk.

"Where will you be staying?" Liz asked Valdez.

"I cannot tell you that, but I will be in touch with you."

"Where should I stay?"

Valdez thought about it for a moment and then said, "A hotel on *Caliente del Sol.*"

"What's the name of it?"

"No name. There is a sign over the door that says 'Hotel'."

"In English?"

"Yes. Many gringos stay there and its owners wish it only to be recognized as a hotel. The people of Mexico City call it the 'Gringo Hotel'."

If it was that kind of hotel maybe she'd also find Tate there.

"What about my friend Gilmore?" she asked.

Valdez looked sheepish and said, "I apologize for the way I reacted yesterday when you mentioned his name. His legendary prowess with a gun is known even here in Mexico. I am afraid I reacted . . . with jealousy."

"Carlos —"

"It was foolish, I know. Of course, if you and Gilmore are willing to help us your assistance will be greatly appreciated. Come, I will take you to the hotel."

"You're going to ride into the city? Don't you have to be careful —"

"I am but a small part of this revolution," he said with a shrug. "I do not have to fear being recognized so easily."

They rode slowly through the streets of Mexico City and Valdez took her to within sight of the Gringo Hotel.

"There is a livery stable just down the street."

"Will I hear from you soon?"

"Yes. I will ask around and see if your Tate Gilmore is in the city."

"I'll be very grateful, Carlos."

"We will talk about how grateful you are later. I must meet with my people. I will talk to you soon."

She watched as he rode away and, as the light

began to fade, she rode toward the hotel. She could already picture the mattress sagging beneath her weight.

Carlos Valdez met with Arturo Fuentes and Felicity Moreno in another part of the city.

"So?" Felicity asked. "How did it go? Will she help?"

"I do not know for certain," Valdez said, "but I believe she can be swayed. What about Gilmore?"

"I did not have an opportunity to bring up the subject with him," she said, "but I can do it tomorrow."

"If you didn't have time to talk, what were you doing?" Fuentes asked, pointedly.

"I was caring for his wound."

Fuentes, who was sleeping with Felicity — when she would let him — looked at her doubtfully, but Valdez spoke before they could start arguing — again.

"How bad was his wound?"

"It could have been worse. I think he will recover if he does not aggravate it. We are lucky that whoever shot him was not a better shot."

"All right," Valdez said, "let's go and talk to the others. We must put our plan into motion."

He rode ahead of Felicity and Fuentes, who argued the entire way. He ignored them, and thought instead about Liz Archer and Tate Gilmore.

Liz stabled Blossom at the livery then walked back to the hotel carrying her rifle and saddlebags. As she checked in she asked the desk clerk if any other Americans had checked in recently.

"Señorita," the man replied, "we have many Americans here. This *is* the gringo hotel."

"So it is," she said. "Thank you."

"*De nada*, señorita." The man was in his early thirties, tall and slender with a very thin mustache. He stared at Liz, obviously liking what he saw and said, "Anything you need, please do not hesitate to ask. My name is Silvio."

"Thank you, Silvio, but right now all I want is a good night's sleep on a nice mattress."

She went upstairs to her room, sat on the bed, and was disappointed to find that the mattress was very thin. Still, it was better than sleeping on the floor.

A few minutes later a knock on her door broke the room's silence. As she opened it she wondered if she would be lucky enough that it would be Tate. But it was the desk clerk, Silvio, holding another thin mattress in his hands.

"I thought perhaps you would be able to use this, señorita." Looking sheepish he added, "Our mattresses are not the best in Mexico City."

He put the mattress on the bed for her, then turned and looked at her wistfully.

"Señorita, perhaps I could stay and help you —"

"That's all right, Silvio," she said, "you've done enough, thank you."

"*De nada,*" he said regretfully and went downstairs to work.

She lay down on the two mattresses, found it only marginally better than having one, and promptly fell asleep.

CHAPTER TWELVE

Tate Gilmore's first three days in Mexico City had been unproductive. He began to think that because of his wound his mind had not been working right.

How could he have thought that simply by coming to Mexico City he would find the man who shot him? Hell, he didn't even know what the man looked like. He had to rely on first finding one of the men who had come out of the bank; *those* men he would recognize. Then he would have to make that man tell him who shot him.

If nothing else, the three otherwise unproductive days had afforded him rest that had benefitted him greatly. He felt stronger than he had since he'd been shot. The only exercise he'd been forced into in the three days was walking the streets of the city, studying faces, looking for one that would be familiar.

He wondered just how much time he should devote

to his mission, but every time he thought about leaving without finding the man who shot him, his temper flared. A man in his position — with his reputation — could not afford to let something like that go unpunished. If he did, then every punk kid with a gun would be after him, thinking they could do it, too.

Tate stopped in a small cafe and had lunch. While he was working on his second pot of coffee, a familiar face walked in.

It wasn't a man, though.

It was Felicity Moreno.

She saw him almost immediately and hurried over to his table. When she reached him she suddenly stopped and became somewhat shy and formal.

"Hello, Tate."

"Hello, Felicity."

She wrinkled her nose and said, "Somehow, it does not sound so bad when you say it."

"Did you come in for lunch?"

"Yes."

"Then sit. I'll have another cup of coffee while you eat."

She smiled and said, "That would be nice."

She ordered lunch and Tate ordered not another cup, but another *pot* of coffee.

"You are looking well," she said, "stronger."

"Thanks to you. What are you doing in Mexico City?"

"I come into the city from time to time to shop. A woman likes to shop, you know."

"Yes, I know."

"We did not really talk much the two days you were at my house . . ."

"No, we didn't," he said, smiling at the memory.

"I did not ask you where you were going, or why. Obviously, you were coming here. Why?"

"Business."

She smiled and asked, "What kind of business — or am I being too nosy?"

"You're being nosy," he said lightly, "but there's no harm in that. I just have to meet a man while I'm here, that's all."

"And then?"

"And then I'll leave."

"Would you . . . consider helping me with a little problem that I have?"

"What kind of problem?"

She stared at him and said levelly, "Saving Mexico."

A mile or so away Liz Archer was walking past a small, stone church and stopped to admire it. She had been walking around Mexico City for the past hour, and although it did not have the sheer size of, say, San Francisco, it did possess an undeniable grandeur.

The church was old and much of the stone was cracked or chipped, but it was still beautiful and it, too, had that same grandeur. She had not spent very much time in churches during her life, but she had an urge to go inside this one. She gave in to it and entered.

The church's interior, if anything, was even more beautiful than its exterior. It was in a state of disrepair, to be sure, but still impressive. Behind the altar hung a large figure of Christ on the cross, and to the right stood a beautiful, smooth, marble statue of the Holy Mother. She approached to get a closer look, and as she did a robed priest stepped through a door to her right.

He was Mexican, and young, perhaps not yet forty. He saw her, smiled, and moved to join her in front of the statue.

"Good morning, my child."

"Good morning, uh, Father."

"She is beautiful, is she not?" he asked, indicating the statue.

"Yes, very beautiful. Your church is very lovely, Father."

"*Gracias.* Of course, it needs some work here and there, but I am doing my best."

"Are you here alone?"

"Quite alone, yes — except on Sunday, of course."

"Of course."

"Is there something I can help you with, my daughter? A problem, perhaps?"

"I have a small problem, Father, but it's nothing that you can help me with."

"Perhaps, if you told me, we would discover that you are wrong."

"I'm looking for a man, and friend who has come to Mexico City recently."

"Another American?"

"Yes."

"And your friend, is he in some trouble?"

"He was . . . shot and wounded some weeks ago, and may not be as strong as he should be."

"Excuse me, my child, but your friend . . . is he . . . a criminal?"

"Oh no, Father, nothing like that. He was trying to

stop a bank robbery when he was shot in the back.''

"Ah," the priest said, "and now he is looking for the man who shot him."

"How did you know?"

He shrugged and said, "It is what I would do — if I were in that situation, of course."

"Of course."

Liz found this priest strange — not that she had known a lot of priests, but this man just did not act like a priest. He didn't talk like one, or more like one —

"You are trying to help him?"

"Yes."

"And finding him here in Mexico City is difficult."

"I do not know where to look."

"Does he know that you are here?"

"He knows that I am coming."

"Then wouldn't he be someplace where you can find him?"

"I suppose . . . but I don't know where to look."

"Think about it, my child," the priest replied, "it will come to you. Please, if I can be of any assistance, come back — and why don't you come to mass on Sunday?"

"I'm not Catholic, Father."

"All are welcome here," he said, spreading his hands. "Good luck in your search."

"Thank you, Father."

"De nada."

She watched as he walked back to the door he had come out of and when he was gone, she looked at the statue of the Holy Mother once more.

Tate would be someplace where he knew she'd be able to find him.

But where?

Another question pushed its way into her mind. From the hang of the priests robes she knew that he had something underneath that was not normally a part of a priest's garb.

Why would a priest be wearing a gun?

CHAPTER THIRTEEN

Tate stared at Felicity, wondering if she were serious or not. From the expression on her face it was obvious that she was.

"That's a bit more than a little problem, isn't it, Felicity?"

"It is," she said, "but perhaps it wouldn't be as big if we had you to help us."

"What can one man do?"

"You are not simply one man, you are the famous American folk hero, Tate Gilmore —"

"I'm hardly a folk hero —"

"You are a famous gunman. Even if people only *thought* you were helping it might make a difference."

"What kind of difference would that make with the Mexican people? You need a Mexican gunman, someone like Johnny Vega —"

"Johnny Vega is dead."

He knew Vega was rumored to be dead because no one had seen him in four years, but he also knew how unreliable were such rumors.

"I meant someone like him."

"We have someone like him, Tate," Felicity said. "We have you."

"Felicity, I have my own problem to take care of."

"Finding out who shot you?"

"That's right."

"We can help."

"How?"

"Since you are here we will assume that the man who shot you is Mexican?"

"I . . . I'm not sure."

"Then why are you here?"

He studied her for a moment, wondering how much to tell her, and then decided to tell her the truth. Maybe she and her people *could* help.

He told her everything that had occurred in Texas and she listened intently.

When he was done she said, "We know that there are . . . overeager patriots who think that the way to raise money for weapons is to cross the border and steal it. We do not approve of these methods."

"You're telling me that these 'overeager patriots' would not be your people?"

"No, I am not telling you that. They could be our people, but if we found that out we would send them away. We don't need those kind of people working with us. Not this time."

"What do you mean, this time?"

"Juarez had those people working for him," she

said bitterly, "and he still does. They are stealing from the people of Mexico, and they must be stopped."

"It seems we're back to square one."

She leaned over her cold, uneaten lunch. "If we deliver the man who shot you, will you stay and help us?"

"Not indefinitely," he said, "and only if I am convinced that you've given me the right man."

"Bueno," she said, standing up. "I will talk with the others and be in touch. Where are you staying?"

"In a hotel called House of the Angels."

She frowned and said, "Why would you stay there? It is used by *putas* and their customers."

He shrugged and said, "One hotel is as good as another."

When Liz returned to her hotel the door to her room was ajar. Drawing her gun she slammed the door open and entered quickly, gun held straight out in front of her.

On the bed Carlos Valdez looked up, surprised, and smiled.

"Do you shoot all the men you find waiting on your bed?" He asked.

"Not all," she told him, "just the ones who surprise me."

She holstered her gun and stepped inside, closing the door behind her.

"What are you doing here?" she asked. She was annoyed bcause she didn't like surprises, especially the ones that made her go for her gun unnecessarily.

"I wanted to let you know that my people have agreed."

"To what?"

"To helping you, in return for which you will help us. You do remember —"

"Yes, I remember. Have you found Tate Gilmore?"

"No, but we are looking now. It should not be too hard to find a wounded gringo in Mexico City — especially someone as famous as he."

"I hope so," she said, walking to the window and looking out. "I don't want him finding the people he's looking for and going up against them alone."

Valdez stared at her for a few moments. "This man means a lot to you?" he asked.

"Yes, he does. He was there in my life when I needed someone, and he has been there ever since."

"It is important to have people like that in your life," Carlos Valdez agreed.

"Yes," she said, still looking out the window but seeing more than the street below, "it is."

Valdez stared at Liz's back, waiting for her to turn around, and when she did not he rose from the bed.

"I will go now. I will be in touch when we have the information you want."

Finally, she turned. "All right, Carlos. I'm sorry if I . . . snapped at you before, or if I seem to be preoccupied."

"You are concerned for your friend's welfare," he replied. "That needs no apology. I will be seeing you very soon."

"I hope so . . ."

CHAPTER FOURTEEN

When Eduardo Soto entered the room the three people waiting there looked up. No love lit up their eyes, but he didn't care. Love was not one of the things he was after. Power was.

"It is about time," Arturo Fuentes said.

"Quiet!" Carlos Valdez snapped.

Soto walked to the table at which they were seated and sat across from Valdez, throwing Felicity an admiring look.

"Nice to see you again, señorita."

"This is not a social function, Soto —"

"Arturo, I will not tell you again," Valdez said, angrily.

"Carlos, this strutting peacock —"

Valdez slammed his hand down on the table and ordered, "Wait outside."

Fuentes wanted to argue, but Valdez's anger blazed

in his eyes and Fuentes decided against it. Valdez had been disturbed when he'd arrived, so something more was spurring anger than just this.

Soto too saw that something was bothering Carlos Valdez.

Fuentes left the room, vowing vengeance for the shame he had just suffered.

"You should have better control over your people, Carlos," Soto said.

"He is ambitious, and impatient. I will control him."

"I'd suggest —"

"I did not come here to discuss my people with you," Valdez said. "Now, suppose you tell us what is happening in the palace?"

"El Presidente grows very disturbed by the increasing unhappiness of his people."

"Ha!" Felicity said. "He cares no more for our happiness than do you. *Maricon*!"

"That is correct, señorita," Soto said to her. "I care most for my own happiness."

"And that is why you are here, is it not, Eduardo?" she asked.

"Yes, it is."

She glared at him and said, "I want you to know that I still do not trust you."

"What must I do —"

"You still might be working for Juarez —"

"Felicity!" Valdez said.

She switched her hot gaze to Valdez and said, "I want him to know where I stand."

Once, Soto had been like them, a revolutionary fighting in the streets for the people. Then, when

Juarez got into office he became a well-dressed, strutting popinjay. She had not liked him before, and liked him even less now.

"We know where you stand."

Soto looked at Felicity and knew where he'd like her to stand — or lie: in his bed! Soon, Señorita, he thought, very soon you will beg to come to my bed!

"How is the plan progressing?" Soto asked.

"As planned," Valdez said. "Both Tate Gilmore and Elizabeth Archer are in the city. We are making sure they are kept apart."

"That is good. Have they agreed to help?"

"Yes, but first we must help them."

"That sounds fair. What do they want?"

"The woman wants to find Gilmore," Valdez said, "and Gilmore wants the man who shot him."

"So give him to him."

"We don't know who it was," Felicity said.

Soto shrugged and said, "What does it matter? Give him someone."

"Who?"

"Anyone," Soto said, and then an idea struck him and said, "Give him Fuentes."

"Arturo is loyal —" Felicity began, but Soto cut her off smoothly.

"He is a fool, and fools are dangerous, even to their own cause." Soto looked at Valdez and said, "I don't care who you give him, just satisfy him so he will agree to help you."

"And then?"

"And then bring him to me. I will do the rest. Who is contacting him?"

"Felicity."

"Ah . . ." Soto said, turning his lecherous eyes to the lovely señorita. "Was it a difficult task to gain his confidence?"

"I have not yet gained it," she said, "but I will. We have become . . . friendly."

"Yes," Soto said, looking at Valdez. "The next time you drag me down to this rat hole I hope you will have more news."

"I am sorry you had · to leave the palace, Eduardo," Valdez said, "but its doors are not yet open to us. You must speak to El Presidente about that."

"I will bring it to his attention," Soto said, standing up.

He left without another word, ignoring the malevolent look that the banished Arturo Fuentes shot him as they passed outside.

Fuentes re-entered the room and started shouting at Valdez.

"Why did you shame me in front of him? You did not have to —"

"Arturo, would you like to kill Soto?"

Fuentes shut his mouth abruptly, then said, "I would like that very much."

"When we have finished with him, you may have him."

"It will be a pleasure."

"Good," Valdez said, "now shut up and let me think."

CHAPTER FIFTEEN

When Soto returned to the presidential palace he was highly sexually aroused. This happened whenever he got excited about something; he believed that Juarez's days as El Presidente were swiftly coming to an end, and this excited him.

The thought of Felicity Moreno in his bed had excited him, as well. Earlier he had told the plump cantina girl to wait for him in his room — in his bed — and he hoped that she was still there. For her sake, she had better be.

He was going to ride her very hard today, and close his eyes and pretend that she was the Moreno woman.

He would also pretend that he was El Presidente.

Both pretenses, he felt assured, would become reality before too long.

Liz lay awake on her double-mattressed bed thinking about Tate Gilmore, and about the time they had spent together since they had met. Surely there was something between them, something they both knew, that would help her find out where he was staying.

Tate was trying to tell her something.

What was it?

Tate Gilmore was lying awake in his bed at the House of the Angels. Staying at a such-named hotel was the only way he could think of telling Liz where he was, but before she could find him she had to find out that there was such a hotel. He could have sent a messenger to her if *he* knew where *she* was, but he didn't.

If she was even here in Mexico City.

Arturo Fuentes and Felicity Moreno had since left the meeting place, but Carlos Valdez was still there when the door opened and the priest stepped in.

"Father Miguel," Valdez greeted him.

"The others?"

"Gone."

"Soto?" the priest asked, distaste plainly marked on his face.

"He was here."

"How are things progressing, Carlos?" Father Miguel asked, seating himself across from the revolution's leader.

"Slowly, Father."

"These two Americans, they are important to the plan?"

"Very."

"I still do not understand how you knew they were coming."

"We have someone in Winfield, Texas, who told us

Gilmore was still alive. A man like that does not take being shot easily. We knew he would come.''

"And the woman?''

"When she appeared in Texas asking questions, and we found out who she was, we knew she would come, also.''

"You did not know their route.''

"We had several routes covered, Father, but Felicity and I took the one most likely. We were lucky.''

"It does not seem right to keep them apart while they are searching for each other.''

"At the end of the week they will see each other.''

"If they are not dead.''

"Liz Archer will not be dead,'' Carlos Valdez said, with feeling.

"You are becoming . . . fond of this woman?'' the priest asked.

"I — I think so, Father.''

"Carlos, you must not let these feelings interfere with your responsibilities to your compatriots and to your country,'' the priest warned.

"I know that, Father.''

"Very well, then I won't press the point. I will leave you to your thoughts.''

As the priest rose and walked towards the door Valdez called out, "Father?''

"Yes?''

"Are you . . . prepared?''

The priest dropped his hand to his right side and Valdez understood that he was wearing his gun beneath his robes.

"I am prepared to do whatever must be done — as we all must be."

The priest left. Valdez stared after him, remembering what Tate Gilmore had told Felicity.

They needed a Mexican legend.

CHAPTER SIXTEEN

The next morning Tate Gilmore was having breakfast in the cafe when Felicity Moreno appeared at his table.

"Good morning, Felicity."

She smiled, but Gilmore could see there was tension in her face and that she was very troubled. Maybe the revolution was not going well. Maybe she had not been able to find out who had shot him.

"What is it?"

She looked at his breakfast and saw that he was almost finished.

"After your breakfast," she said, "could we go to your room?"

"Sure," he said, taking a hasty last sip of coffee. "Sure, come on."

"But . . . you're not done."

"I am now," he said, taking her by the elbow and leading her outside.

On the way to his room he asked, "Have you found the man yet?"

"After," she said, "we can talk after . . ."

It was more enjoyable this time than it had been at her house — for him, anyway — because he was stronger and able to participate more fully. Still, they finished with her sitting astride him because she still worried about his wound.

"That was wonderful," she sighed, lying next to him with her arm draped over his chest.

"Did it get rid of any of the tension?"

"No," she said, honestly, "but I do feel better. I'd feel even better if we never had to leave this room."

"Felicity —"

"I know," she said, placing her hand flat against his chest, "I know."

His right arm was around her and his left throbbed from his shoulder down to the wrist — but he didn't tell her that. He had been on top of her for a short time, supporting his weight on both arms, and now the left one was protesting.

"Is this all you wanted to see me about this morning?" he asked.

"No," she said.

He waited while she decided whether or not she wanted to tell him.

Finally, she said, "We have found the man."

"The one who shot me?"

"Yes?"

"How?"

"We asked," she said, simply. "He was very proud of what he did and spoke up without urging."

"What did you do to him?"

"Nothing," she said. "We decided to leave that up to you."

"Where is he?"

"We will arrange for you to see him before the week is out."

"Why that long?" he asked impatiently.

"Tate," she said, propping herself up on one arm, "we need him just a little bit longer."

"For what?"

She looked as if she didn't know how to answer that, then repeated, "We need him. We ask you to let us have him just a little bit longer. At the end of the week I will tell you where to go to meet him."

He thought about it and then said, "All right. If that's the way it has to be."

"There is one more thing," she said, putting her head on his chest now.

"What is it?"

"Can I come here again?"

"Sure," he said, rubbing his hand over the silky flesh of her back.

"Every morning, until the end of the week?" Before he could answer she added, "I need you to keep me from going crazy, Tate."

"Why don't you get out of it, Felicity?"

"Walk away from the revolution?"

"Sure," he said, "why not?"

"And do what? Go where? Back to the United States, with you?"

"Uh —"

"Do you have a woman?" she asked, suddenly.

"Uh, not really —"

"But there is someone."

"Yes," he said, thinking of Liz. They had never really said as much to each other, but he felt he could answer that question honestly in the affirmative.

"And she would not like it if I came back with you, would she?"

"Felicity —"

"It is all right," she assured him. "I cannot go with you, anyway. My place is here, with my people, doing what I can do to save my country."

"I suppose so . . ."

"All I need from you is the rest of this week," she said, sliding her hand beneath the sheet and finding him. "That is all . . ."

"You've got it."

She kissed his chest, pausing to run her tongue around each nipple, while holding onto his penis, which was swelling rapidly.

Sliding on top of him and rubbing her furry patch up and down the length of him she said, "Perhaps by the end of the week we can change positions, no?"

He slid his hands up her back and said, "Maybe even before then . . ."

CHAPTER SEVENTEEN

Liz's breakfast was also interrupted that morning, by the appearance of Carlos Valdez.

"Carlos," she said, looking up surprised. "I didn't expect to see you so soon."

"May I sit?"

"Please. Have some breakfast?"

"Perhaps some coffee."

They were in the hotel dining room, which was so small it had only one waiter. She beckoned him over and told him to bring another coffee cup.

"*Sí*, señorita," he said, staring at her in frank appreciation.

"Do you get used to that?" Valdez asked her.

"Get used to what?"

"Men looking at you like that."

The question made her uncomfortable, and she shifted in her seat.

"I guess so — I don't know."

"You are very beautiful," he said, "and with your blonde hair you would be ever more desirable to Mexican men."

"Like you?" she asked, trying to make *him* uncomfortable now — and failing.

"Yes," he said, "like me."

The double mattress did absolutely nothing to quiet the squeaking of the bed, but after a few moments they were totally unmindful of it. All that concerned them was each other, and their present need for each other.

Liz blamed a few things for that: being in a strange place, not knowing if Tate were alive or dead, indecision about what to do . . . she just wanted to forget everything for a little while, and Carlos Valdez was there . . . and he *was* attractive and a very good lover.

"We wasted a lot of time between the first time and now," Valdez said.

"Carlos —"

"I know," he said, putting his finger to her lips, "I'm sorry I said it. Never mind."

"What brought you back so soon?" she asked. "Certainly not this."

"Yes, this," he said, "though not *only* this. We think we have found the man who shot your friend."

"Is he still alive?" she asked, misunderstanding at first. She thought that he meant that they had found Tate.

"The man who shot him is, yes. We have not yet located your friend, however."

"I see. Well, where is he?"

"We have a problem there."

"What kind of problem?"

"We can't give him to you," he said, his tone apologetic. "At least, not yet."

"Why not?"

"We need him."

"For what?"

"There is still something he has to do for us, something important to the revolution."

"When, then?"

"At the end of the week," he promised. "I'll tell you where to find him at the end of the week."

She thought a moment, then said, "Well, if that's how it has to be. How did you find him so fast?"

"We asked around and he confessed. He was proud of having shot down an American legend."

"He won't be so proud when that American legend finds him."

"Or even another American legend."

"I'm not a legend."

"Perhaps not," he said, "perhaps in the future men will tell your story as a . . . a fable."

She made a face and said, "I think I like 'legend' better."

He slid his hand up over her belly and ribs until he cupped one large breast and said, "I like you no matter what you are called."

"I'm just a woman," she said, turning in bed to face him, "just a woman . . ."

"A woman, yes," he said, "but never 'just' . . ."

CHAPTER EIGHTEEN

Felicity Moreno left Tate Gilmore's room feeling confused. When Carlos Valdez had first approached her, telling her that an American was on his way through Mexico, an American who could be very important to them, she agreed to help. She allowed Valdez to set her up in that house out in the middle of nowhere, because it actually *wasn't* really nowhere. It was along the most likely route that the American would take to Mexico City.

She had been out there alone for many days, thinking about her life — she was only twenty-five, though she knew she looked older — and about the revolution. The revolution that had put Juarez in power had taken the lives of her father and her brother. Her mother had died soon after, simply because she didn't care to live anymore. By the time the American had appeared she was prepared to do anything for the revolution, but he had been so attractive to her that sleeping with him was something she did because she wanted to, not because she had to.

Now, suddenly, the American and sleeping with him was all she thought about.

This confused her.

After Felicity left, Tate dressed slowly, thinking back over the past few weeks. He'd been feverish a lot of the time, unable to think straight, at least not the way he should have. That meant that he hadn't been asking the questions he should have been asking.

Once, idly, he'd wondered what Felicity had been doing at that house out in the middle of nowhere. And what of the coincidence of their meeting here in Mexico City?

He was willing to bet that there was more to Fecliity Moreno than what he had seen.

He'd keep his eyes and mind opened a little wider from now until the end of the week.

Carlos Valdez's confusion was much the same as Felicity's. His feelings for Liz Archer were alien to him. For a long time he had cared about nothing but his country. Yes, he had slept with women from time to time — Felicity more than any other — but he'd never felt anything for them like what he felt for Liz.

For the first time in his life — a life that had been fraught with danger — he was frightened, because he didn't understand what was going on inside of him.

After Carlos Valdez left her room, Liz sat up in bed and wondered again about him. She still didn't trust him, but not because she thought he was a bandit. She was convinced now that he *was* what he presented himself to be, a revolutionary who cared about his country and his people — but she was an American, and she did not think that he would be above using her to gain freedom from Juarez for his country.

Even if he felt deeply for her she would always have to take second place to his country.

And that was the way it would be with her, she mused, if it were *her* country that was in conflict.

She really wouldn't be able to blame him if he was trying to use her, but at the same time she was going to have to try and make sure that he didn't succeed.

She'd have to keep her eyes opened extra wide from now until the end of the week.

CHAPTER NINETEEN

The day passed uneventfully. The night did not.

Liz was awakened that night by the sounds of shots in the street. She got up and went to the window but all she could see were confused figures running pell-mell in the street and the occasional flash from a gun. She dressed, strapped on her sidearm, and went downstairs.

Silvio, the desk clerk, was on duty and when he saw her coming down the stairs he moved to intercept her.

"Señorita, you do not want to go out there." He blocked her path with his body, but he was so slender she felt she could have moved him with a sweep of her arm.

"Why? What's happening?"

The man made a face as if he'd just bitten into a rotten piece of fruit. "Juaristas. They are cleaning the streets."

"Cleaning the streets? Cleaning them of what?"

"Rebels."

"How do they know who's a rebel and who isn't in the dark?"

"They don't," Silvio said. "They just shoot anything that moves."

"That's crazy."

"It is a lesson for the people."

"What if there are children on the street?"

"Then they hide," Silvio said. "Juaristas don't care if they shoot men, women or children. To them, they are all the same: rebels."

"That's crazy."

"Ah, to be a Juarista you have to be crazy, because Juarez, he is crazy."

"Was he crazy before he became President?"

"*Sí,*" Silvio said with a shrug, "but then, nobody ever noticed."

Liz walked to the door but did not go out. Every so often someone would run by, followed by a Juarez soldier on horseback. There were shots, and once she heard someone scream.

Then she saw the little girl out in the center of the street. She couldn't have been more than seven or eight years old.

"What the hell is she doing out there at this time of night?"

Silvios moved alongside of Liz and looked out, then made a clucking sound with his tongue.

Suddenly, the sound of many horses rang out through the night.

"Juaristas, a lot of them," Silvio said.

"The little girl . . ."

Shaking his head Silvio said, "They'll ride her down as a rebel."

The little girl was just standing there, looking up at the sky.

"Why doesn't she move?"

"She is as good as dead."

"No, she's not."

"Señorita . . ." Silvio shouted, grabbing for her, but she was out the door and gone.

Outside the sound of the horses was even louder as they came toward the little girl. Liz ran into the street, caught up the little girl in her arms and kept running. The Juaristas rode by so fast that she could have sworn they never saw her, but a couple who were trailing did.

Three Juaristas, riding at the end of the column, spied her holding the little girl. They stopped and turned their horses to face her. She stood just off the boardwalk, holding the child at her side with her left hand.

"Is that your child?" one of them asked.

"No."

"What are you doing with her."

Liz raised her chin defiantly and said, "Keeping, you and your horses from trampling her."

"Is that child Mexican?"

"No," Liz lied, but the little girl chose that moment to say something in Spanish that Liz didn't understand.

"Shh," she said, pushing the child behind her, but it was too late.

"Take the child," the Juarista said to his companions.

"That's just what you're going to have to do," Liz called out, "take her from me."

"Señorita, you are American and perhaps ignorant of our laws. The child is a rebel —"

"That's ridiculous! How can a child be a rebel?"

"She is out after dark," the man replied. "That makes her a rebel."

"Then by that definition," Liz said, "you and your men are rebels, too."

"Enough talk." The man ordered his companions, "take the child *and* the woman."

"Don't get off your horses!" Liz warned.

The spokesman finally lost his patience and his temper.

"Kill them both . . . now!"

All three Juaristas went for their pistols; Liz drew and fired. Her first shot caught the spokesman just below his nose, knocking his head back. He slid off the horse and fell limp to the ground.

Her second shot punched one of the other men in the chest, knocking him off his horse. His horse then backed into the other man's horse, inciting it to rear and leading Liz's third shot to miss its mark. Instead of killing the man the slug struck him in the shoulder, causing him to drop his gun. Using his uninjured arm he turned his horse's head and rode off after the rest of his patrol.

Liz holstered her gun, picked up the little girl, and walked back to the hotel.

"Leave her with me," Silvio said, reaching for the child.

"Why?"

"You must get away. That man will bring back the

rest of them. You are branded a mercenary in the
employ of the rebels now that you have killed two
Juaristas. You will have to go into hiding.''

"I can't go into hiding —"

"You must, or you will be killed! With that blonde
hair you will be very easy to find."

"Is the little girl all right?"

"She's fine."

"Ask her."

The man looked exasperated, but bent over and
asked the little girl in Spanish if she was all right.

"She says she's fine and wants to know if she can
touch your hair."

The little girl's hair was very dark, and Liz bent
over so she could touch her own blonde hair.

"Muy bonita."

"She says it's very pretty."

"Tell her so is she."

He relayed the message and then insisted, "You
must get out of here!"

"And go where?"

"I will tell you where to go," he said impatiently,
"but you must get your things and go now."

"All right," she said, "all right. You'll take care of
the little girl?"

"I will," he said, "I promise."

"I'll get my things."

Silvio gave Liz an address and instructions on how to
get there and — after she made him promise again to
take care of the little girl — she left.

Liz kept to the shadows, watching for Juaristas,

and wondered how the hell she was going to find Tate Gilmore now if she had to stay in hiding.

Silvio had been right about one thing. It was going to be pretty hard for her to travel during the daytime with her blonde hair.

She managed to get to the location Silvio had given her without being spotted — ducking into doorways on two occasions to avoid Juaristas — and she knocked on the door. She had to knock twice before it was answered.

"Qué pasa?" a woman's voice asked through the closed door.

Liz guesed she was being asked what she wanted, or who she was.

"Silvio sent me over."

She heard a bolt being thrown and then the door opened a crack. There was no light and she could only barely discern the face that peered out.

"Why?"

"I killed two Juaristas tonight."

A pause, and then, "Why?"

"They were going to trample a little girl as a rebel. I couldn't let that happen."

Another pause, and then the door opened wider.

"Come in, quickly."

Liz stepped inside and the door was closed behind her, and bolted. As she waited a match was lit, and then a candle. The woman holding the candle appeared to be in her early thirties, a very handsome woman with long, dark hair.

"Como se llama?" the woman asked, then translated, "What is your name?"

"Elizabeth Archer."

"Silvio is my cousin," the woman said to her. "If he sent you here — and if you killed two Juaristas — you are welcome here."

"Thank you."

"I will show you where you sleep . . ."

She followed the handsome woman down a long corridor that had been sectioned off on both sides into wooden cribs, with flimsy wooden doors. They were much like the cribs that prostitutes used when they couldn't afford to work the hotels.

"Who are in these?" she asked.

"Other rebels, people on the run," the woman said. "This is one of the places where they hide when the Juaristas are out in force, like tonight."

Liz thought about asking what the charge would be, but then decided that would just insult both the woman and her cousin, Silvio.

"This is yours," the woman said, stopping before a door. "You can keep it for only one night."

"That's fine."

As Liz opened the door the woman added, "It will cost you five American dollars."

Liz looked at the woman and thought, so much for insults.

CHAPTER TWENTY

"A woman!" President Juarez roared. "A woman killed two of my soliders and drove off another?"

"*Sí*, El Presidente," said Captain Julio Sanchez.

Sanchez was very frightened because Juarez was livid, his face suffused with blood, and he was pacing back and forth behind his desk like a caged tiger.

"How?" El Presidente demanded. "Why? Explain to me how this could happen to three of your men, Sanchez."

"*Sí*, Excellency. M-my man said that they were trying to take in a rebel and this — this woman opposed them. When they attempted to arrest her, she began shooting at them."

"And why did they not shoot back?"

"They were taken entirely by surprise, Excellency, and . . . and she was . . . very fast with the gun."

"Bah! A woman!" Juarez said, and then he suddenly thought of something and grew calm. The Captain was used to his President's mercurial changes of mood, and was extremely grateful for this one.

"What did she look like?"

"My man says she was very beautiful, Excellency, hair the color of the sun, and a fine, full, womanly figure. She looked like an angel, he said, but she wore a gun on her hip and used it with the speed of a devil!"

Juarez thought this over for a few moments and Sanchez waited, shaking inside, wondering what was coming. Punishment, physical abuse . . . or death?

When Juarez finally spoke his tone was deceptively mild.

"Sanchez, get me Soto. Tell him I want him here — immediately."

"*Sí*, Excellency."

Sanchez backed out of the room, fighting his urge to run. He didn't know how or why, but it seemed that El Presidente's ire was about to be transferred to his aide, Eduardo Soto.

And it couldn't happen to a nicer man, Sanchez thought with glee.

"Tell me about this woman who is supposed to help us rout the rebels, Soto," Juarez said.

The president of Mexico was sitting in his chair, regarding Soto as if he knew something his aide did not. This made Soto very uncomfortable.

"Tell me about her, I am very interested."

Soto was confused, but thought that it would be best to humor the man.

"Her name is Elizabeth Archer, Excellency, known

in the United States as 'Angel Eyes,' " he began, then changed his tack. "But I have told you all of this, Excellency. Why are asking about her?"

"Sanchez was just in here, Soto," Juarez replied. "He told me that two of my Juaristas were killed last night, and another wounded."

"I don't understand," Soto frowned. "You have had men killed before, Excellency."

"Not by a woman!" Juarez shouted, leaning forward and pounding his fist on the desk. "A blonde woman, very beautiful and very fast with a gun. Does that description fit anyone we know, Soto?"

"Angel Eyes."

"Very good," Juarez said sarcastically. "Now would you mind telling me why she is killing my men when she is supposed to be here helping me?"

"Excellency, I said she was going to be a help to us," Soto said, "I did not say that she would willingly help us."

"You are speaking in riddles, Soto. Riddles give me headaches," Juarez warned.

"Please, Excellency, you have left this matter in my hands."

"I want her to pay for killing my men."

"They were probably incompetent."

"Which does not say much for her, does it?"

Immediately, Soto realized that he had taken the wrong tack, and tried to recover.

"Forgive me, Excellency. I should have remembered that El Presidente does not employ any incompetents."

Eyeing Soto very deliberately Juarez said, "I would not be too sure of that, Soto."

"Excellency —"

"Very well!" Juarez pointed a finger at his aide. "Handle it then, but remember, the consequences are on your head. I do not want to hear of this woman killing any more of my men. Is that understood?"

"It is understood, Excellency."

Juarez lowered his voice, but his words had a bite just the same.

"If you would spend more of your time doing your job, Eduardo, and less time fucking whores, you would be much better off, don't you think?"

Gritting his teeth Soto said, "As you say, Excellency."

Soto went back to his apartment where the chunky cantina girl was still waiting. She was apparently very content to stay in his bed until he wanted her, rather than go back to work. Well, he was tired of her, so she would be going back to work very shortly.

But first Eduardo Soto had to purge himself of his anger and frustration, and the cantina girl was the closest target. He dared not see Valdez while he was in this mood. Valdez was as stubborn as he was and Soto knew that they would end up butting heads. In such confrontations no one wins, Soto knew. When he went to see Valdez he had to be calm and in control.

If a cantina girl had to suffer a little pain for that to happen, so be it.

CHAPTER TWENTY-ONE

"Did you hear what happened last night?" Arturo Fuentes asked Carlos Valdez and Felicity Moreno.

They were in a cafe on a small side street, one that fed rebels for free. Fuentes sat down and asked the waitress to bring coffee.

"What happened?"

"That woman of yours killed two Juaristas."

"What?" Felicity asked, jarred.

"She shot down two Juaristas last night."

"How do you know this?"

"I heard it from Silvio's sister."

"Is that where she is?" Valdez asked. "At Silvio's sister's?"

"That's where she spent the night."

"What happened?"

"She took a child from the Juaristas."

"Juaristas!" Felicity spat. "They would kill a child and call it a rebel."

"It was a little girl," Fuentes said, accepting the coffee from the waitress. "Your lady friend did her good deed, Carlos, and now she has to stay out of sight. That blonde hair of hers will make her very easy to find."

Valdez stood up. "Where are you going?" Feuntes asked.

"To get her. Silvio's sister will be charging her by the night — if she lets her stay past the first one."

"Where are you going to take her?"

Valdez looked at both of them in turn as they waited for the answer and said, "Only I will know."

When he left Fuentes looked at Felicity and grinned.

"He's going to take her to church."

Liz was getting ready to leave when Valdez arrived at the front door.

Silvio's sister let him in and he saw the money in Liz's hand.

"Put that away."

"Carlos —"

He turned to the handsome woman and said, "You will not take her money, Consuelo."

"Silvio says I must always —"

"I will talk to Silvio," Valdez said. He took Liz's saddlebags and rifle from her, then took hold of her arm and walked her outside.

The exchange between Valdez and Consuelo had taken place entirely in Spanish, and all Liz had understood was Valdez's anger, and Silvio's name.

Outside Liz asked, "What was that about?"

"That Silvio, he has houses like this set up all over the city. He sends people who are in trouble here and has his sister charge them to stay. She tells them they can stay one night, then charges them twice as much to stay a second night."

"If you know he does this why do you let him go on?"

"Because he supplies shelter for these people," Valdez said, "but I *am* going to have a talk with him, as soon as I get you to safety."

"Where are you taking me?"

"Someplace safe. We will have to stay on the rarely travelled streets and alleys. That blonde hair . . ."

"I thought you liked my hair."

"I do," he said, "and I want you to keep it."

They had walked quite a few blocks when she finally said, "Come on, Carlos, where are we going."

He looked at her and said, "We are going to church."

"This is it," Valdez said.

They were standing at the side of a church. She looked up and realized it was the same church she had been inside earlier in the week.

"I've been here before."

"You have?"

"Yes, it's a very pretty church."

"It needs fixing."

"That's what the priest said."

"You met the priest?"

"We didn't exchange names or anything, but we talked."

"Well, I will now introduce you properly."

He started toward the church and she grabbed his arm.

"The priest is a rebel?"

Valdez hesitated and then said simply, "He helps."

He took her by the arm and led her into the church by a side entrance.

"Father!" he called out.

The church was darkened but she was able to make out some movement from the back, near the altar. A figure walked toward them and she recognized he was the same priest she had earlier spoken with.

"You are back," he said.

"Yes."

"And Carlos," the priest said. He looked back at Liz and asked, "Is this the friend you were looking for?"

"No, but he's going to help me find him."

"Is that true, Carlos?" the priest asked, looking at Valdez.

"This is Liz Archer, Father Miguel," Valdez said. "She needs a place to stay for a while."

"Oh? Why?"

"She had some trouble last night."

Father Miguel kept looking at Valdez, waiting for more.

"With Juaristas."

The priest stared and then suddenly his face brightened. "I heard that five Juaristas were killed by one person last night. A woman." He peered at Liz and asked, "Was that you?"

"It was," she admitted, "and it wasn't five. It was two."

"It was three, actually," Valdez said, "but one was only wounded."

"It wasn't my fault —" she started, but Father Miguel interrupted her.

"You don't have to justify yourself to me, my child," he said. "I understand there was a child involved? A little girl."

"Yes."

"And you saved her life."

"I suppose . . . yes, I did."

He took her hand and said, "Then you are welcome here for as long as you like."

"It won't be too long, I hope, but thank you."

"Carlos —"

"I must be leaving, but I will be back later. Take care of her, Father Miguel."

"God will take care of her, Carlos."

Sure, Liz thought, as Carlos left, God and Father Miguel's gun.

CHAPTER TWENTY-TWO

"What happened?"

"If you didn't know what happened, Eduardo, you wouldn't be here."

Valdez and Soto stared at each other while the waitress cleared the table before them. They were at the same cafe where Valdez had had breakfast with Felicity. Valdez hoped Soto would not wonder why they were not meeting at the church.

"I know what happened," Soto said when the waitress left. "What I would like to know is how, or why? What did she think she was doing?"

"She thought she was saving a child from Juarez's animals. A small child, Eduardo."

"You are breaking my heart, Carlos."

"You are as much of an animal as he is, Eduardo."

"So," Soto said, sitting back, "we will sit here and call each other names. Fine."

"No, we will not sit here and call each other names. You will stand up and go *and* you will leave everything to me."

"She is useless to us now, you realize that, don't you?" Soto said. "She would never have a chance of getting near Juarez."

"Then we will use her friend Gilmore," Valdez said. "One is as good as the other."

"Gilmore," Soto said, staring over Valdez's shoulder. "Where is he now? Do you know?"

"Yes."

"Don't let anything happen to him," Soto said, pointing a finger. "I mean, don't let him kill anyone until we're ready to use him."

"Soto," Valdez said, "get out of here and let me do my job."

Soto stood up. "Do this right, Carlos. Don't let him slip through your fingers. Make sure he does what we want him to do."

"How do you suggest I do that?"

"Well, since you asked," Soto said, "just let him know that you have something he wants — or some-*one*."

"Tell me something, Eduardo," Valdez said, spying the skinned knuckles on the man's hands.

"What?"

"Are you still beating up whores for fun?"

"No, Carlos," Soto replied, "not just for fun."

"Father," Liz said.

"Yes?"

They were sitting in the sacristy and the silence had became awkward. She decided to ask the question that had been burning in the back of her mind since the first time they had met.

"Why do you wear a gun?"

He looked at her and smiled.

"I don't usually."

"Why now?"

"Times are difficult, my child. We must all be prepared to do what we can, what we must."

"And you expect that you will, at some point, have to use a gun?"

"It will not be the first time I have used a gun, Liz," he said. "It will, however, be the first time since I became a priest."

"When was that?"

"About three years ago. Before that I sort of wandered around aimlessly for a year."

"And before that?"

"I don't like to think about the time before that."

"May I see the gun?"

"Of course."

He raised his robe, revealing the gun in its holster, and then removed it and handed it to her.

"I've never seen a gun like this before," she said, holding it in her right hand.

"It's English, a forty-five caliber Deane-Adams five-shot revolver."

She handed it back, even more confused than before. What would a priest be doing with such a gun?

She decided to probe.

"Does something puzzle you?" he asked.

"If you'd rather not talk about it —"

He waved her words away and said, "We are cooped up here together, so why not talk?"

She had no idea what was coming next, so she waited curiously.

"Have you ever heard of Johnny Vega?"

"Of course," she said. "He is reputed to be Mexico's fastest gun. Some say he was as fast as Hickok."

"Was?"

"Yes, he's dead."

"No," Father John Miguel de la Vega said, "I am not dead."

Liz was stunned for a moment, and then found her voice.

"You are Johnny Vega?"

"I was Johnny Vega," he said. "I am now Father John Miguel de la Vega, which is my real name. As a young man, however, looking to make a reputation with a gun, I did not like the way that sounded, so I became 'Johnny Vega.' "

"Well . . ." she said, at a loss for words after that.

"So, your question should now change," he said, helping her out. "Rather than wondering why a priest carries a gun, you should ask how a gunman becomes a priest?"

"H-how?"

He shrugged.

"Johnny Vega became disillusioned with himself. Suddenly, beating men to the draw and killing them was not the thrill it once was. Oh yes," he said in response to the look on her face, "I did it for the thrill. You've killed people yourself. I know your reputation."

"But I don't find any thrill in it."

"Of course not. Finding a thrill in killing is a sickness."

"Which you had."

"But I got better," he pointed out. "When I realized what I had become I think I went into shock. I travelled about for almost a year until I came to a church. There I found peace and a friend in Father Franco. I went to the seminary and became a priest, and I went back to that church."

"This church?"

"Yes."

"And Father Franco?"

"He was dead when I got here."

"How?"

"Killed by the Juaristas as a rebel sympathizer."

"And was he?"

"Yes."

"And that's why you're helping the rebels?"

"Partly. I'm also doing it because this is my country, and I want the best for it."

"When you went to the seminary did they know about your past?"

"Yes," Father Miguel said, "all of it."

"And they still made you a priest?"

"If God forgives," Father Miguel continued, "can man attempt any less? I was told there it didn't matter what I once was, only what I would be, what I wanted to be."

"And now? Will God forgive you now that you've put on your gun again?"

"I hope so," the priest said. "As I said, I would only use it if there was no other choice."

"I hope that situation does not arise, Father. You've straightened out your life, and killing again could only ruin it for you."

"I would have a choice to make if it did," Father Miguel said. "My God or my country."

"I guess that would be a pretty hard decision for a priest to make."

"A hard decision for any man, Liz, not just a priest."

Suddenly she realized that there must be a lot of temptations involved in being a priest. She realized at that moment he was looking at her, not the way a priest looks at a woman, but the way a man does.

Valdez stayed at the cafe after Soto left, thinking about the last thing the man had said. The man had suggested that by telling Gilmore they were holding Liz Archer they could get him to do what they wanted him to do — to kill Juarez.

Of course, Carlos Valdez had no intention of harming Liz Archer, but Tate Gilmore would have no way of knowing that.

Meanwhile, Liz would be at the church waiting patiently for them to find Gilmore for her.

When it was done, once Juarez was dead, then they could allow Gilmore and Liz to get together and leave Mexico — except for one thing.

Carlos Valdez didn't want Liz Archer leaving Mexico with Tate Gilmore, or anyone else. He wanted her to stay here with him, but as long as Tate Gilmore was alive he knew she wouldn't consent to that.

So, not only would Tate Gilmore have to kill Juarez, but the Juaristas would have to kill Gilmore, as well.

After that, Liz Archer would be his.

Eduardo Soto thought that he had handled pretty well the imbroglio set off by Liz's shooting the Juaristas — and perhaps what the girl did might actually work to his advantage. Now they would turn away from Liz to Gilmore. And Soto would have more confidence in Tate Gilmore than he would in *any* woman, no matter what they called her.

As for Juarez, it was satisfaction enough to Soto that El Presidente was upset at having two of his men killed by a woman.

And speaking of a women Soto needed a new one. He'd gotten a little carried away with the cantina girl and he hoped that his men had carried her out by now.

He didn't want to bring a new woman up there and have her scared off by a dead body.

Soto had worked his way out of the small streets and alleys to where his coach was standing and was about to climb aboard when he heard his name called out. He turned and saw Arturo Fuentes.

"What the hell do you want?" Soto demanded.

Putting a disarming smile on his face Fuentes said, "I want to talk."

"About what?"

"We don't like each other, Soto, but I would like

to talk about something that will be mutually reward-
ing to us — and we could still go on disliking one
another.''

Soto knew that Fuentes would turn in his own
mother for a reward — if there was a reward, and if
he had a mother. Soto had no doubt that what
Fuentes now had in mind was betraying someone a lot
less close than a mother — namely Carlos Valdez.

"All right, Fuentes," Soto agreed, "let's talk . . ."

CHAPTER TWENTY-THREE

Later that day Carlos Valdez once again met with Fuentes and Felicity and told them about the new arrangement. They were meeting this time in a different cafe, though one much like the first one, small and out of the way.

"I don't like it," Felicity said.

"Why not?" Arturo Fuentes asked. "Because you have to lie to your precious Tate Gilmore?"

"I think we could get him to help us willingly," she said to Valdez, ignoring Fuentes.

"We can't take any chances, Mike," Valdez said. That alone made Felicity suspicious, because he never called her Mike. Rather, she always had to tell him not to call her Felicity.

"Whose idea was this?"

"It was mine."

"I don't believe you, Carlos. You don't want to lie to Liz any more than I do to Tate."

"Come now, Felicity," Fuentes cut in, "both of you have already done your share of lying to both Gilmore and Miss Archer. Why stop now, just when you're getting so good at it?"

She turned to Fuentes and said hotly, "This sounds more like something you would think up."

"Not me," Fuentes said, "although I wish I had. It's actually a very good idea."

She glared at both men for a few moments. "Soto," she guessed then. "This is Eduardo's idea, isn't it?"

"I agreed," Valdez said quickly. "It is the only way to ensure that Gilmore will do what we want."

"And we are not going to use Liz?"

"She has become a liability. She would be instantly recognized by the Juaristas. She must remain in hiding until we are finished."

"And will she agree to this?"

"She will have to."

"And who will be assigned to guard her and make sure she doesn't get away — without her knowing she is being guarded, of course."

"Someone reliable."

"You have already begun your plan, haven't you!?" she said, suddenly.

"What do you mean?"

"You took her to Father Miguel, didn't you?"

"Enough!" Valdez said, standing up and slamming his hand on the table.

There were a few other diners in the cafe who looked up, attracted by the commotion.

Valdez sat down and said, "It will be done this way, and that is that."

"Fine with me," Fuentes said jauntily, but Felicity continued to fume.

"Felicity, you will have to tell him."

"I don't —"

"Felicity! This is a revolution, and in a revolution you must do what you are told if you wish it to succeed. You do wish it to succeed, don't you? You do want to rid our country of Juarez, don't you?"

"Yes, yes, yes! All right, I will do it."

"I am asking you only to do it," he said, trying to ease her mind, "not like it."

"Oh, I will not like it, I assure you — and neither will Tate Gilmore. Have you thought about his possible reaction to this news. What if he kills me?"

"He won't."

"What if he kills you, or Fuentes?"

"He doesn't know about us, does he?"

Felicity waited a moment and then said, "No, he does not."

"And you will not tell him, Felicity," he said, reaching for her hand across the table, "because you are a good soldier. Is that correct?"

"I don't want to be a soldier anymore," she said. "I would like to be a normal woman again."

"Soon," Valdez said, "that time is coming very soon."

Tate Gilmore was lying on the bed in his room, listening to the noises that filtered through the thin walls from the next room. A prostitute had brought her customer up there twenty minutes ago and the two were stilll doing it. He could hear the man's moans and the girl's cries, and he knew that the girl was faking for the man's benefit. She was the most active of all the House of the Angels whores, and her performances never varied. Well, at least the men enjoyed it.

There was a knock on his door and he thought it might be that pretty little whore again. This young, dark-haired whore had taken an apparent liking to him and had already knocked on his door twice today, asking if he was lonely. He was no lonelier now than he had been either of those times, but she had to be told. He only hoped she wasn't still wearing that peasant blouse, the one that showed off her pointed little breasts.

When he opened the door there was a dark-haired woman there, all right, but it wasn't the little whore.

"Felicity."

"May I come in?"

"This is no place for you to be."

"The hall is not," she agreed, "but it seems fairly safe in your room. May I?"

"Of course."

He stepped aside to allow her to enter and then closed the door.

"It's nice to see you."

Her back was to him and she didn't turn when she began to speak.

"You won't think so when you hear what I have to say."

"What is it, Felicity? What's wrong?"

She turned now to face him and said, "We have Liz Archer."

"You found Liz?" he said, misunderstanding. "That's wonderful. Where is she?"

"No, you don't understand what I am saying, Tate," she said slowly, painfully. "We — I mean, the others, they're holding her as a hostage."

"Hostage? For what purpose?"

"They want you to do something for them, and after you do it you will both be free to go."

"And what is it they want me to do?"

"I will let them tell you," she said, starting for the door. "I'm supposed to bring you to them, now."

As she passed by him he grabed her roughly by the arm and spun her around to face him.

"I'm not going anywhere until you tell me something, Felicity. Where is she?"

"I don't know."

"Then what is it they want me to do? Tell me!" he said, shaking her.

"They want you to kill him."

"Kill who?"

"The president, El Presidente. Tate, they want you to assassinate Juarez."

He released her arms and studied her, looking into her eyes for a long time.

"Well, shit," he said finally, "and I thought it would be something hard. Come on, lead the way."

CHAPTER TWENTY-FOUR

The light was fading as Felicity Moreno led Tate Gilmore down some sparsely populated streets. He was fairly certain he wasn't being led to his death. He decided that if she had wanted him dead she could have done it any one of half a dozen times earlier. However, that didn't stop him from stretching his fingertips to the butt of his gun now and again, just to make sure it was still there.

Finally she led him to the door of a small cafe.

"Aren't you coming inside?"

"No. There is a man in there waiting for you. His name is Carlos. He will explain everything."

She started away but he stopped her with his hand on her arm.

"You don't like this, do you?"

"No."

"Come and see me soon, Felicity, and we'll talk. All right?"

She looked up at him, only fleetingly meeting his eyes, and said, "Yes, all right."

He released her and she left, almost running. He entered the cafe.

It was empty but for the man sitting at a back table; no waiter or waitress was in sight. The man at the table appeared to be in his early or middle thirties. He was hatless, revealing a patch of curly, black hair, and his dress was that of a bandit, bandoliers across his chest. He was not a bandit, though; he was a rebel, a revolutionary, and potential hero to the people of Mexico.

"Tate Gilmore?" the man said aloud. His English was accented, but Gilmore had no difficulty in understanding him.

"That's right."

"I am Carlos."

"Good for you."

"Please, come and sit down."

As Gilmore approached the table a waiter emerged from a curtained doorway in the back.

"Just coffee," Gilmore called out before the man came too far into the room, and the waiter turned and went back through the curtain.

Gilmore faced the man and asked, "Do you mind if I sit there, that chair?"

The man looked surprised and pointed out, "There are three other chairs."

"I would rather sit with my back to the wall."

The man called Carlos — it made no difference whether that was his real name or not — shrugged, rose, and shifted to the next chair.

Gilmore moved around to claim the empty seat,

from which he could see the rest of the room. He leaned his right shoulder against the wall, careful to keep his left off it.

The waiter came in with a pot of coffee, and placed it and an empty cup in front of Gilmore.

"Gracias," he said, and the waiter bowed slightly and left. Gilmore took his time pouring the coffee before he spoke.

"What's this all about?" he asked Carlos. "Have you found the man who shot me?"

"That is not why you are here."

The man's stare was flat and hard, and Gilmore could have sworn that even though they'd never met, the man disliked him intensely. Or maybe he just hated gringos.

"I told Felicity I would not help you unless I found the man who shot me."

"You no longer have a choice."

Hard glare. They were going to play a game, it seemed, to see who was the harder man.

"What does that mean?"

The man suddenly looked sad as he said, "We have Elizabeth Archer."

"You . . . have her?" Gilmore repeated, enunciating very carefully. "What exactly does that mean, you *have* her?"

"We are holding her . . . prisoner," Carlos said, for obvious want of a better word, "until you do what we want you to do."

"Kill President Juarez."

"Yes."

"That's crazy."

"It's necessary."

"If it gets out that the president of Mexico was killed by an American it could start trouble between the two countries. Is that what you want?"

"We want Juarez dead. You are the man to do it."

"I don't understand," Gilmore said. "Why me?"

"We decided that it would be either you or Elizabeth Archer — Angel Eyes — but last night she was forced to kill two Juaristas. She is too easily recognizable, and they now will be looking for her."

"Has she agreed to this?"

"She did not know about it, and still does not."

"Where is she?"

"She is safe."

"How did you decide on us?"

"We did not . . . decide. After you survived the shooting in Texas we knew that you would come here. Later, we discovered that she was following you."

"So you decided to make use of us."

"Yes, one or both."

"So it's both. You're using her to get to me."

"Yes."

"What makes you think I'll agree?"

"You will. You . . . care for each other."

"You know that for a fact?"

"Yes."

There was no way to bluff the man. It was obvious that he had spent time with Liz and *knew* that she and Gilmore cared for each other. The knowledge that Liz and the man had spent time together made Gilmore think there might be a reason that the man had such dislike for him.

"I'll have to think about this."

"Of course. Go back to your hotel and think about

it. We will send someone for your answer
tomorrow.''

Gilmore rose, leaving the cup of coffee untouched.

''Send Felicity.''

''No,'' Carlos said, shaking his head, ''we will send
who *we* choose.''

Gilmore decided not to argue. Felicity would come
to him, anyway. He felt sure of that. She was against
this, and that might be something he could use.

''All right.''

''Please, Señor Gilmore,'' Carlos said, ''I do not
wish any harm to come to L — Miss Archer.''

''I believe you.''

''Then believe this, as well,'' the man said carefully,
as if he wanted to make certain he was not
misunderstood. ''She *will* come to harm if you do not
cooperate.''

''I believe that, too,'' Gilmore said, ''but you
believe this —''

Carlos held up one hand and said, ''There is no
need for threats.''

''Let me get this off of my chest, anyway.''
Gilmore leaned on the table so that his face was very
close to Carlos's. ''If anything does happen to her,
I'm going to kill you. That's a fact.''

Carlos matched stares with Gilmore, finally
swallowed, and said, ''I believe you.''

''Good,'' Gilmore said, straightening up. ''You'll
have my answer tomorrow.

CHAPTER TWENTY-FIVE

Leaving the cafe Gilmore got lost trying to find his way back to his hotel. He thought he remembered the twists and turns that Felicity had taken, but along the way he must have taken a wrong turn.

Once he thought he was almost on the right trail when he passed a small stone church that had seen better days, though still it had an imposing presence. He was almost disposed to go in but decided against it. He wanted to get back to his hotel because his back was beginning to hurt again and his wound to ache, and he wanted to get into bed where he could relax and think this through properly.

Inside the church Father Miguel spread out three queens with a triumphant grin.

"Not again!" Liz wailed.

"The Lord is guiding my hand."

"You mean he's guiding *my* hand," Liz corrected. "I dealt that hand."

"What does it matter whose hand he is guiding? The important thing is that I am winning."

"How much do I owe you now, Father?"

"Not me, my child, the church — and I believe you owe us several thousand dollars."

"Well, deal them out again. The night is young and I could still win it back — along with a few trinkets from the altar."

"Never!" Father Miguel said, shuffling the cards.

"I've never met a priest like you, Father. You carry a gun, you play poker well, you look —" She stopped short when she realized what she'd been about to say."

"I look . . . what? What were you going to say?"

"Nothing . . ."

"Come on, it must have been something."

"I — well, I was just going to say that you . . . look at me like a man would, every so often, instead of like a priest should."

"And are you an authority on how priests should look at beautiful, desirable women?"

"No, but —"

"Are we supposed to be half dead and not notice?"

"No, but —"

"Or are we supposed to avert our eyes for fear of turning into a pillar of salt like Lot's wife?"

"Of course not —"

"Then tell me, Liz Archer, how am I supposed to look at you?"

"I . . . don't know, Father. Could we, uh, just play cards?"

Laughing, Father Miguel dealt the cards and announced, "Five card stud . . ."

Carlos Valdez's first meeting with Tate Gilmore told him that the man was deadly. It was only because Valdez knew Gilmore was wounded that he noticed the slight stiffness when he moved, otherwise there was no outward indication that the man had been so severely wounded such a short time ago.

A man like that, who could carry such pain without showing it, was dangerous. His eyes, too, carried the same message of danger. There was no expression in them when they spoke of Liz Archer, yet Valdez knew that Gilmore cared for her. By the same token, Valdez knew that he had not been able to keep emotion out of *his* eyes when he spoke of her, and he knew Gilmore had seen that, too.

Still, they had Liz in a safe place, and there was no way Gilmore could find out where she was unless someone told him.

A thought struck Valdez then, an uncomfortable thought.

Unless someone told him . . . like Felicity.

Back in his hotel Gilmore bent to take off his boots and pain shot through his shoulder. He yanked the boot off brutally and threw it at the wall, shouting, "Goddammit!"

He was angry because he was not completely fit at a time when Liz Archer's life might depend on him. And how many other lives? . . .

Juarez.

Felicity!

Jesus, if Felicity's dissatisfaction with the situation was plain to him, it would be painfully obvious to the rebels. They had Gilmore where they wanted him as long as he didn't know where Liz was . . . and the only person who might tell him was Felicity.

He stood up, one boot on and one boot off, and looked around the room. He felt helpless, because he knew now that Felicity's life too was in danger and he had no idea how or where to find her.

Two women's lives depended on him, and he was . . . impotent!

CHAPTER TWENTY-SIX

Felicity didn't know where to go.

There were several "safe" places she could spend the night, but none held any attraction for her tonight. What she wanted was to go to Tate Gilmore's hotel, tell him everything, and stay with him. She wanted to forget about Juarez, the revolution, everything . . .

She stopped walking suddenly and listened. She was in a narrow alley not far from one of the rebel "safe" houses, and she thought she heard someone behind her?

Juaristas?

No, they would not be so subtle. Those animals would ride down the alley at full speed and try to trample her beneath their horses' hooves.

She started to walk again, slowly, alert; then she heard a boot scrape.

She turned, her hand reaching toward the small pistol she kept in her belt, and shouted, "Who is it?"

No answer.

"Who's there?"

Still no answer.

She pulled the gun out and cocked the hammer.

"I have a gun, and —"

"Easy, Felicity, take it easy," said a voice she recognized.

She peered into the darkness as the figure approached.

"Arturo?"

"Si, Arturo, mi amor," the man said. He came closer and she was able to see his face. The tension left her body and she put her gun away.

"You frightened me."

"I am sorry, Felicity," he said, "I did not mean to frighten you."

"Where are you going?" she asked.

"I was looking for you, *querida*," he told her softly.

"Me? why? Oh, please, Arturo, tonight I am not in the mood."

She had slept both with Arturo and with Carlos at other times, but that had not happened recently. At one time she was excited by both of them, but neither man held any attraction for her anymore.

Now there was only Tate . . .

"Felicity."

"I have asked you not to call me that!"

"As you wish," he said, coming closer, "Mike . . ."

She saw the moonlight glint off the blade much too late to do anything about it. Fuentes' hand came forward and the knife entered her belly cleanly, as if her skin were made of butter.

Her shock kept her from initially feeling the pain. She grunted as if she had been punched in the stomach, and then Fuentes turned the blade so that it was pointing up and slicing through her, opening her wide.

She felt the pain as she fell, but then it was gone . . .

As the knife entered her stomach Arturo Fuentes experienced a surge of excitement. His penis had become engorged, rigid, and when he ripped the knife up through her bowels he almost climaxed in his pants.

He had never before killed a woman that he had once made love to.

He stared down at her as she lay on the ground, aware of the painful erection throbbing in his pants. He leaned over, wiped the knife off on her pants and put it away. He reached for her pants and unbuttoned them, yanking them down around her ankles.

Then he did the same to his own . . .

Less than half a mile away Carlos Valdez sat with his head in his hand.

He was a coward.

Of course he knew what Arturo Fuentes would do when he told him what he thought about Felicity and Tate Gilmore.

"She cannot be trusted," Fuentes had said.

"Perhaps," Valdez had said, but when Fuentes left he knew exactly where he was going, and what he would do.

As he sat with his head in his hands he wondered how long it would take Fuentes to figure out that if Felicity couldn't be trusted with Tate, perhaps Valdez couldn't be trusted with Liz . . .

CHAPTER TWENTY-SEVEN

The day before it happened . . .

In the morning Tate stood up from the bed, still with one boot on and one boot off, and walked to the window to look out at the street below. But there was no sign of Felicity.

The whore next door had set a new record for men serviced in a single night, and now he could hear her through the wall, snoring loudly. She was getting her well-deserved beauty sleep.

He had hoped that Felicity would come to him last night, and then his hope switched to the morning. He wondered now who Carlos would send for his answer, and he wondered even more what his answer would be.

Of course, it was obvious. He would have to agree to anything they wanted until he was able to find out where Liz was and get her to safety. Of course, since she *was* Angel Eyes, there was always the possibility that she would get herself to safety. There was also the possibility that they did not actually have her, and that she was not even in Mexico City . . . but he couldn't take that chance.

He sat back on the bed and forced his second boot on. He removed the shirt he had slept in all night, washed his face and chest with water from the pitcher and basin, and then put on a fresh shirt. He went downstairs then, intending to have breakfast at the nearest cafe where whoever Carlos sent could still find him.

Liz awoke and for a moment did not know where she was — then she remembered. She was in a small room at the rear of the church, barely large enough for her and the pallet she was sleeping on. There *was* a small wooden table against the wall, with a pitcher and basin on it, which she used to wash. Then she changed her clothes and went outside to find Father Miguel.

She had managed to win back most of her money in the poker game last night before they decided it was time to turn in. Now she wanted to find out from the priest what was going to happen today. She hoped that Carlos Valdez would come back and fill her in on what was going on. She wanted to tell him that she had no intentions of staying cooped up here indefinitely, Juaristas or no Juaristas. She still had to find Tate and help him.

"Ah, you are awake," Father Miguel said as she entered the church.

"Good morning."

"Come into the sacristy and have breakfast with me."

"I want to talk to you —"

"We can talk there. Come, you must be hungry."

She could smell the coffee he had made and discovered that she was indeed hungry.

"All right, Father. Thank you."

She still had trouble accepting this mild-mannered priest as the former Mexican gunman Johnny Vega. Vega was still a legend in Mexico, a legend made ever more compelling by his unexplained disappearance. If he stepped forward now, as Johnny Vega and not as Father Miguel, the people were sure to follow him wherever he would lead — even if it were to the presidential palace itself.

She wondered what plans Valdez had for the priest, if any — or if *he* even knew that Father Miguel and Johnny Vega were the same man. No, that was silly. He had to know, didn't he?

Father Miguel had prepared eggs and biscuits to accompany the coffee. Liz wolfed them down.

"It was careless of me not to have offered you something to eat last night."

"No, that's all right," she said, honestly. "Last night I didn't notice my hunger."

"I can prepare more if you like . . ."

"No, thank you, Father. I'll just have some more coffee . . ."

He poured it for her, and then set about clearing the table.

"Father," she said when he finished, "I'm going to have to leave —"

"You can't," he said, quickly.

"What?"

"I mean, Carlos will be here soon. I'm sure he wants to talk to you today."

"That's fine, Father, but if he doesn't have the information I need today I'm going to have to go out and try and get it myself."

"I'm sure he will be able to help you . . ."

Liz wished she was as sure as the priest seemed to be. She was beginning to have her doubts that Valdez ever wanted to help her find the man who had shot Tate Gilmore, or even Tate himself.

A man fighting for his country would never hesitate to do what he thought was right, no matter who it hurt.

She had to keep that in mind.

Carlos Valdez awoke from his nightmare with a start. Immediately, the plot of the nightmare was gone, leaving behind only the terror it had brought.

He stood up and thought about Liz, hoping that she would not become impatient and try to leave the church. Johnny — Father Miguel — would have to stop her, then.

He thought about Felicity, forgetting for a moment that she was dead. Fuentes had returned late last night and, although no words passed between them, the look on Fuentes' face told Valdez all he needed to know.

Now he had to decide who was going to go to the House of the Angels and get Gilmore's answer. He couldn't send Fuentes, because he'd probably end up antagonizing Gilmore, who might just kill him —

although that itself wouldn't be *so* bad. No, he'd probably have to do it himself, after he talked to Liz. He was going to have to tell her something to satisfy her and keep her from leaving the church.

All he had to do was think of something.

Eduardo Soto awoke in an empty bed, feeling oddly satisfied with himself. The day of reckoning was so close at hand that he decided not to replace the cantina girl so quickly.

When he was El Presidente, he would be able to replace her with a woman of substance, and not with just another cantina whore.

Juarez awoke in his sumptuous apartment in the palace and wished he were back in the mountains with his *compadres*. Being El Presidente was not all that he had hoped it would be. Instead of being grateful for having a strong leader, the people were trying to kill him.

In the mountains, when he was the rebel leader, people were trying then to kill him too, but they came at him from the front, and not from behind like cowards, trying to knife him or shoot him in the back.

CHAPTER TWENTY-EIGHT

Father Miguel was at the altar when Carlos Valdez walked in, and motioned the rebel leader to come over.

"Where is she?" Valdez asked.

"In the sacristy," Father Miguel said. "She is very impatient and wants to leave."

"You have to keep her here, Johnny."

"Father Miguel."

"Yes, of course, Father Miguel."

"How do you suggest I do that, Carlos?"

Valdez leaned over and patted Father Miguel's gun through his robes.

"I can't do that."

"Well, I know she's faster than you, Johnny, but —"

"That is not what I meant!"

"No?"

"I have never pointed my gun at a woman."

"What is so bad about pointing your gun at a woman? You don't have to shoot her."

"What if she insists on leaving?"

"She can't leave, Johnny!" Valdez said loudly.

"Do not shout in the Lord's house."

"Well, she can't!" Valdez hissed.

"What are you going to tell her?"

"I don't know," Valdez said, "but I will tell her something."

"It had better be something good."

Valdez backed away from the altar and walked toward the sacristy.

Liz was sitting at the table staring at the wall when he entered.

"Liz . . ."

She looked up, focused on him and said, "Carlos, what took you so long?"

"I had some . . . things to take care of."

She stood up and said, "I need my man, Carlos, or I'll have to go out and find him myself."

"You can't go out, Liz. The Juaristas are looking for you."

"It will be their misfortune to find me."

"Liz —"

"Carlos, where is the man who shot Tate Gilmore? And where is Tate Gilmore?"

"I will bring them both to you . . . tomorrow."

"Why tomorrow?"

"The man who shot Gilmore is not in Mexico City yet. He will be arriving tomorrow."

"And Tate?"

"Gilmore is trailing him."

"You mean Tate knows who he is?"

"Yes, and he's after him."

"With his wound he's out trailing this man?"

"Your friend Señor Gilmore is a very determined man."

"I've got to help him —"

Valdez took her by the shoulders. "The best way you can help is to stay here at the church with Father Miguel," he said. "Tomorrow both Gilmore and the man who shot him will be in Mexico City."

Staring at Valdez she said, "Carlos, I hope you aren't lying to me."

In that moment, Carlos Valdez knew he was looking not at Liz Archer, but at the legend called "Angel Eyes".

Tate Gilmore was walking back to his hotel from the cafe when he spotted Carlos Valdez ahead of him. He quickened his pace to catch up.

"If I can recognize you, so can the Juaristas. I thought you were going to send someone to talk to me."

Valdez looked at Gilmore, surprised, and stopped.

"Keep walking," Gilmore said, and they continued on.

"I thought I should come and talk to you myself."

"To let me know that you've released Liz Archer?"

"Not quite. I hope you do not think that I enjoy doing this, but it must be done."

"Why don't you do it yourself, then?"

"I could not get in to see El Presidente."

"And I can?"

"Much easier than I, or any Mexican. Juarez is suspicious of all Mexicans now."

"His own people."

"Yes, but he knows that most of his people would gladly kill him."

"How will you get me in to see him? . . . if I agree to this, that is."

"It will be arranged."

"And Liz?"

"When you are finished you will be brought directly to her."

"Let's go in here," Gilmore said as they passed a cantina.

They went inside, bought a couple of beers and sat at a back table.

"I don't like being turned into an assassin."

"Please, señor," Valdez said, "your reputation is well known even here in Mexico."

"As what? Certainly not as an assassin."

"Perhaps not, but you *have* killed many men."

"Never in cold blood. They were either trying to kill me, or they truly deserved to die."

Valdez raised his eyebrows and said, "I did not know that your reputation included being judge, jury, and executioner — or should I just say God?"

"I'm just a man trying to live his life, señor," Gilmore cautioned, "and you are interfering in that."

"I aplogize, but I am just a man trying to save his country. What would you do for your country, señor?"

Gilmore felt compelled to answer honestly. "Anything."

"Can I do less?"

"But forcing people —"

"Enough of this debate, señor. Will you or will you not do it?"

"If you tell me that her life depends on it, then yes, I'll do it." Gilmore leaned forward. "Are you telling me that, Carlos?"

The man hesitated long enough for Gilmore to feel that his heart wasn't wholly in this.

"That is what I am telling you — and it won't have to be me who kills her, Gilmore. There are others who would be quite willing to do it. Do you understand?"

"I understand that you're telling me you can't control your people."

Thinking of Arturo Fuentes, Valdez said, "That is what I am telling you."

They stared at each other for a few long moments and then Gilmore said, "All right, I'll do it."

Valdez finished his beer and stood up.

"I will come for you tomorrow."

"What's tomorrow?"

"You have an appointment to see El Presidente Juarez."

CHAPTER TWENTY-NINE

"Tate Gilmore is here."

"At the palace?" Juarez asked.

"In the city," Eduardo Soto said. "He will be here at the palace tomorrow."

"What for?"

"You need a bodyguard, Excellency, one of this man's . . . capabilities."

"I am touched by your concern, Eduardo."

"I am thinking only of your welfare, Excellency, and the welfare of the people."

"The people are who I need a bodyguard from."

"They will realize soon that you are a great leader, have no fear."

"And this Gilmore will keep me alive long enough for them to do that?"

"Yes."

Juarez stared at Soto and said, "Very well, I will

talk to him. I will decide if he will be my bodyguard or not."

"As you wish, Excellency."

Valdez left the cantina and met Arturo Fuentes a block away.

"Keep watching him, Arturo."

"I will make sure he doesn't go anywhere," Fuentes said, touching the knife in his belt — the one Valdez was sure he had used on Felicity.

"Just watch him, Arturo," Valdez said. "I don't want anything to happen to him."

"Not until after he kills Juarez, eh?"

Valdez glared at Fuentes and said, "That is right."

When Gilmore left the cantina and started back to his hotel he spotted the man almost at once — and he didn't think it was an accident. The man wanted Tate to see him, and to recognize him for what he was. He was tall and blade thin, twin bandoliers crossing his chest and a wicked-looking knife thrust in his belt. The man might now call himself a rebel, but for most of his life he had been nothing but a bandit — and a killer.

Valdez had left the man there to watch Tate — but why? As long as they had Liz he wasn't going anywhere — unless he could find out where she was, but how could he do that?

There was still a chance that Felicity was alive to tell him, but he seriously doubted it. Perhaps this man was the very one who killed her.

Valdez must have a motive for sending this man to watch him, Tate reckoned.

Whatever his reason, Valdez might thus have given Gilmore the means to find Liz.

As he reached his hotel Tate continued walking, looking for a likely alley in which to hold a meeting . . .

Soto left Juarez's office rubbing his hands together. The plan was now in motion. Juarez was obligingly going to allow the man who would kill him into the palace.

He was hiring his own killer.

Juarez walked to his office window and sneaked a look outside. It was unwise to stand by the window too long — an old bullet hole in the glass attested to that fact.

He dwelt on having a gringo bodyguard and the more he thought of it the better he liked it. A Mexican bodyguard always might take it into his mind to become patriotic and decide to kill Juarez rather than guarding him.

A gringo, on the other hand, could feel no such surge of patriotism. Instead, he would simply work for whoever paid him — and who could pay him more in Mexico then El Presidente himself?

Valdez watched Gilmore walk past his hotel, and watched as Fuentes followed him. He felt sure he could rely on Feuntes to try something stupid and get himself killed.

Which would save him the trouble.

CHAPTER THIRTY

Finally, Gilmore found an alley he liked and walked into it. Flattening himself against the wall of the building he waited. The trailing Mexican walked right in. Gilmore grabbed him by the shirt front and drove his knee into the man's stomach; the man gagged and went down to one knee. But Gilmore wasn't finished. He had too much anger built up inside — and who could tell, maybe this was the sonofabitch who shot him.

He half-dragged the man further into the alley, then flung him sprawling and kicked him in the side. The Mexican tried to curl up to avoid further damage, but Gilmore stepped behind him and very deliberately kicked him in the right kidney.

The man was tough. He hauled himself to his hands and knees and Gilmore could see that he was reaching for the knife in his belt. He grabbed a handful of the

Mexican's greasy black hair and yanked his head back far enough that the man cried out in pain. Then he grabbed the man's own knife and put the point right underneath his chin.

"You and me are going to have a talk now, amigo," he hissed into the man's ear.

"No comprendo, señor," replied the Mexican.

"Oh, you comprendo all right, friend, because if you don't you're no good to me and I'll just slit your throat right now."

He yanked on the man's hair and positioned the knife blade across his throat. Gilmore was panting from the exertion and his left shoulder ached.

"No, wait —" the man cried out in English.

"You understand me, right?"

"Sí, señor, I understand."

"That's fine. You're going to tell me where Liz Archer is, aren't you?"

"I cannot, señor. If I do they will kill me."

"And if you don't I'll kill you. Die now or die later, amigo."

"Please, señor . . ."

"Make up your mind!"

When the man didn't reply right away Gilmore cut him just enough so that the blood started dripping down his neck.

"The church, señor, she is at the church!"

"What church?"

"The Church of the Sacred Heart."

"Tell me how to get there."

The man babbled out the instructions and Gilmore realized that it was the same stone church he had seen the day before.

"All right, you're doing real good so far, amigo. Just two more questions. Who shot me in Texas —"

"Señor?"

"And who killed Felicity Moreno?"

"Señor?"

"If she wasn't dead she would have come to see me this morning. Somebody killed her and I want to know who."

"Señor, I can tell you who shot you."

"Is that a fact?" Gilmore asked. The Mexican's eagerness to answer *that* question told Gilmore the answer to the other one.

"Who?"

Arturo Fuentes said a name, and Gilmore believed him. He also believed without a doubt that this was the man who killed Felicity Moreno.

What was it Valdez had called him: "Judge, jury, and executioner?"

Well, why the hell not!

"I can't take this waiting anymore," Liz said to Father Miguel.

"Didn't Carlos tell you —"

"I know what Carlos told me, Father, but I don't know that I believe it. Gilmore should have gotten to Mexico City before I did, no matter how slowly he travelled."

"Perhaps he was here and left again?"

"No, he would wait for me."

"Where?"

"As you said, it should be somewhere he knew I'd find him."

"Have you been able to think of such a place?"

"No."

"Then I suggest you wait for Carlos."

"I haven't seen Felicity or Fuentes around. What happened to them?"

"I don't know about Felicity, but I would not be surprised if Fuentes is out visiting some of the local whorehouses. Or perhaps choosing a girl from the streets."

"Where do the girls take their customers from the streets of Mexico City? To hotels, or are there cribs?"

"There is no need for cribs," Father Miguel said, "not while there are hotels like the House of the Angels and The Hotel del Gato —"

"Wait! What did you say?"

"Hotel del —"

"No, the first one."

"The House of the Angels? It is very popular with the street whores —"

"Where is it?"

"A few miles from here," he said, describing that area of the city.

"That's it," she said, standing up. "That's where Tate is."

"Why do you say that?" Father Miguel asked, eyeing her carefully.

"Angels, House of the Angels!" she pointed out to him excitedly. "Don't you get it? Angel Eyes — House of the Angels?"

"That is very imaginative —"

"No, it's not, it's where he is. I have to go, Father —" she said, heading for the door.

"Liz!" he shouted.

She turned and saw him standing, his robe pulled away from his gun.

"You can't leave."

She turned to face him straight on.

"*Can't* leave?" she repeated. "That makes it sound as if I'm a prisoner."

"I do not want to put it that way, but —"

"Father — or are you Johnny Vega, now?"

"I am Father Miguel."

"Then I don't think you're going to want to draw and fire that gun in the Lord's house."

He looked indecisive for a moment, then said, "I would have to follow you outside."

"Father, I don't want to fight you. I am not a particularly religious person, but I would feel terrible having to shoot a priest — even one who is an ex-gunman."

"Please," Father Miguel said, "wait for Carlos —"

"Carlos has been lying to me, hasn't he, Father? All along?"

"I . . . cannot speak for Carlos. I can only say that he is doing what he thinks is best for Mexico —"

"You can't use people, Father, not even in the name of patriotism. Now, you're either going to use that gun, or I'm going to leave. Which is it?"

They locked glares for several tense moments, and then Father Miguel dropped his robe over his gun.

"You would probably beat me, anyway," he said, "I am very rusty."

"I'm glad to hear it," Liz said, breathing easier. "I'm sorry, Father, but I've got to go."

"I understand."

"I hope this doesn't cause you trouble with Carlos."

"No trouble. My help is voluntary. I am not one of his rebels. *Vaya con Dios*, Liz. Go with God."

"Thank you, Father."

Following Arturo Fuentes' directions Tate Gilmore found his way back to the Church of the Sacred Heart and arrived there just minutes after Liz Archer had left. He found Father Miguel in the sacristy.

"You are Gilmore?" Father Miguel asked.

"Yes, Father. I'm looking for a blonde woman."

"Yes, Elizabeth Archer."

"You know her then?"

"Oh, yes."

"Was she here?"

"She was, but she is no longer."

"Where did she go?"

Father Miguel may not have been able to draw his gun for his country, but he hoped that the Lord would forgive him for lying for it.

"They took her from here."

"Where?"

"I do not know that, my son. I am sorry."

Thinking that the priest was simply a bystander in all this, Gilmore accepted his word and left the church, apologizing for having bothered him.

"It was no bother, my son. I hope you find her."

After Gilmore left Father Miguel went into the church to confess.

When Liz Archer arrived at the House of the Angels

Hotel she asked the desk clerk for Tate Gilmore's room number.

"That crazy American?" the clerk asked.

"Why is he crazy?"

"Who else but a crazy American would stay in a hotel like this, señorita?"

"Well, is he in his room?"

"No, señorita, he went out early this morning and has not returned."

"Damn."

"Señorita?"

"Yes?"

Smiling at her and eyeing her appreciatively, he asked, "Would you like a room?"

"No, thank you."

"I could make a special price for you."

"Thanks, but no. I'll just go up and wait in my friend's room."

"As you wish."

She went up to the second floor, passing a scantily clad Mexican woman hanging onto a drunken man in the hallway, haggling over price.

She found Gilmore's room, opened the door and stepped in — and felt the barrel of a gun pressed against the back of her head, behind her left ear.

"Carlos?"

"Yes, it is me," Carlos said. He reached around and took her gun before she could get any ideas.

"How did you know?"

"I saw your friend kill Fuentes, and I knew that Fuentes would tell him where you were."

"Tate went to the church?" Liz asked, closing her eyes.

"I am sure he did."

"What made you think I would come here?"

"I took a chance," Carlos said. 'I did not think I could beat him to the church, and did not have time to gather more of my people to stop both of you from escaping. I took a chance that Father Miguel would let you get away."

"And if he hadn't?"

"Then you and Gilmore would be gone, and I would have to devise a new plan for Juarez's death."

"Well, why don't you do that, anyway, and just forget about us?"

"Because it can still work," he said. He took hold of her arm and said, "Now come, we must find someplace to keep you until it is all over."

On the way to the rear exit they passed the same whore, still haggling over her price.

When Gilmore returned to his hotel he asked the desk clerk if anyone had been asking for him, on the off chance that Carlos — or even Liz — had been there in his absence.

"Yes, señor, a lovely señorita was looking for you."

"Señorita? What did she look like?"

"Ay, *muy bonita*, señor, with golden hair — and very odd, she wore a gun. Such a woman is made for beds, not guns, no?"

"Yes. Where did she go?"

"Up to your room."

"How long ago?"

"An hour, maybe."

"Thank you."

Gilmore took the stairs two at a time and burst into his room only to find it empty. He looked around, but could find no evidence that Liz was ever there . . . except for the scent in the air. It was hers.

She *had* been there, and now she was gone!

Did Carlos have someone else watching the hotel, and if so, why?

There was a knock on the door and Gilmore moved quickly to open it.

"Liz —" he said, but it wasn't Liz Archer. It was his friend, the dark-haired little whore.

"Are you perhaps lonely today, Señor?"

"No, not today," he said, hastily. "I'm sorry."

"I thought since your woman had gone away with another man that you might be lonely," she said, turning away.

"Wait, what did you say?" he demanded, stepping out into the hall.

"Your woman, the blonde one, she left with another man."

"You saw them?"

"*Sí.* I was . . . conducting business in the hall. I saw her come up and go into your room, and then she and another man came out."

"Did you see the other man go in?"

"No, señor."

"What did he look like."

She described Carlos Valdez.

"This is very important, so please think hard. Did she go with him willingly?"

She thought a moment, and then said, "Well, he

was holding her by the arm with one hand, and I could not see the other. He had it behind her.''

Probably with a gun in it.

''There was something else I noticed.''

''What?''

''She was wearing a gun when she went into your room, but when they came out she had only an empty holster.''

That was it, then. Carlos had her and Gilmore was back to square one.

''All right, thank you, señorita,'' he said, digging into his pocket for some money. ''Here.''

''*Gracias*, señor. Are you sure you are not lonely?''

''I'm sorry.''

''So am I. *Buenos tarde, señor.*''

Gilmore went back into his room and sat on the bed. He had run around the city for nothing. Liz had been right here waiting for him. If only he had been here . . .

Wait a minute.

The priest said that they had taken her away from the church, but if she had been here that meant the priest lied and probably knew more than he was saying.

He started to leave, then sat back down again. The man was a priest and probably a rebel sympathizer, but that didn't mean he'd know where the rebels were holding Liz.

He stood up again and went out the door.

There was no harm in asking.

CHAPTER THIRTY-ONE

The next morning there was a knock on his door, much heavier than that of the pretty little whore. Gilmore opened the door and found two Juaristas standing in the hall.

"Señor Gilmore?" one of them asked.

"That's right."

"We are to take you to the palace, señor."

"That's very nice of you."

As he stepped out into the hall the spokesman asked, "Would you give up your gun, señor?"

"No more than I would give up my right arm," Gilmore said, facing the man squarely.

He watched the man's eyes and knew he would back down — he also knew that he had been ordered to back down. Whoever Carlos' inside man was, he was a good one.

"Shall we go?" he said to the Juaristas.

"This way, señor."

Outside he found a buggy and climbed aboard. One Juarista got in the driver's seat, and the other mounted a horse.

The grandeur of Mexico City was dwarfed by that of the palace itself. Immense, magnificent, constructed of stone and adobe, it looked like a fort — and he was going to walk right in.

To kill Juarez.

Liz had spent an uncomfortable night.

Her hands and feet were bound and she was lying on a bed made of stacked burlap sacks. Her back was stiff; her hands and feet were numb.

The door to her room opened and a man stepped in. He was one of the two men with whom Valdez had left her the night before.

"Señorita, do you want some breakfast?" he asked in heavily accented English.

She didn't really, but she was hoping that he would untie her hands to let her eat so she said, "Yes, very much."

"Bueno," he said. He stepped out of the room momentarily, leaving the door open, and came back carrying a tray.

He set the tray on a wooden table and then moved towards her.

She lifted her hands to be untied but instead he stooped, lifted her effortlessly, and then carried her to the table, sitting her down on a straight backed chair.

"Aren't you going to untie my hands?"

"I am not supposed to, señorita."

"How am I to eat like this?" she demanded, raising her bound hands.

"I am sorry —"

"For Christ's sake, man, I'm not going to hurt you."

Stung by the implication that he might be afraid of her he took out a knife and neatly cut her bonds.

"Do not try anything, señorita, or I will not be the one who gets hurt."

"I just want to eat my breakfast."

"Then eat," he said, striding from the room. She listened and heard the bolt thrown home. She pushed away from the table and began to untie her feet. As she did so she heard angry shouts from the next room, and then the sound of a door banging open.

She had her feet untied when she heard the bolt thrown back, and she hastily pulled herself up to the table and pretended that she was eating.

The door opened and a voice said, "Come along, señorita."

She turned and saw Father Miguel.

The two Juaristas walked Tate Gilmore up the front steps of the palace right through the front entrance, past the guards. Just inside a man waited, a well-dressed Mexican in his thirties who appeared to be somewhat nervous.

"Señor Gilmore?" the man asked.

"Yes."

"My name is Soto, Eduardo Soto. I am El Presidente's aide."

"Good for you."

"Yes, well," Soto said. He turned to the Juaristas and said, "You may go."

They saluted, turned, and walked away.

Gilmore stared at Soto, wondering if this was Carlos' man inside the Palace.

"I will take you El Presidente's office. He will interview you for the position as his bodyguard."

"Bodyguard," Gilmore said. "All right, fine."

"Come with me, then."

Soto led the way and Gilmore followed. They climbed a winding staircase to the second floor, far above the first. Gilmore kept waiting for Soto to turn and give him some kind of message that would identify him as a rebel, but the man just kept walking, down a long, wide, high-ceilinged hallway toward a set of huge double doors.

"This is the president's office," Soto said, stopping before the doors.

"I could have guessed."

He waited, but Soto made no attempt to say anything else to him.

"Do you have something else to tell me?"

"Like what?"

Gilmore shrugged and said, "A piece of advice."

Soto stared at him and said, "Your reputation will probably get you the job, Señor Gilmore. I have no advice that will help you."

"Uh-huh, okay, thanks."

Soto knocked and opened both doors.

"Excellency, Señor Gilmore is here."

"Ah, good, good. Bring him in."

Soto stepped aside and Gilmore walked in. When he saw Juarez the first thing he thought of was a bear.

Not that the man was as big as a bear, but he was solid and he exuded brute power. He appeared to be in his fifties, with grey-streaked hair and beard, and looked as if he'd be much more at home on a mountain with bandoliers crossing his chest.

"I will leave you alone to conduct your interview, Excellency," Soto said. "I have other matters to attend to."

"Fine, go, go. I want to talk to Señor Gilmore alone."

"I will leave a man outside in the hall to show him out."

"Fine."

Soto withdrew and closed the double doors.

Gilmore looked at Juarez and marvelled at how easy it had been for him — a potential assassin — to get into the president's office. He could have pulled his gun at any time now and shot the president of Mexico.

"Come, come, have a seat. I will give you a drink. What would you like? I have whiskey."

"That will be fine.

Gilmore approached the president while Juarez poured two drinks. As he reached the desk Juarez handed him a drink and toasted, "To the revolution."

Gilmore was sure that he meant the revolution that put him in power, and not the present one. It was obviously an old toast.

"Now," Juarez said, putting down his empty glass, "we should talk."

"Yes," Gilmore said, drawing his gun, "we should."

Outside the president's office, in the hall, Eduardo Soto stood with four Juaristas, poised to burst into the room at the first sound of a shot.

He was holding his breath.

"I don't understand," Liz said, as she followed Father Miguel, who was setting a torrid pace. "Where are we going? Why did you let me out? I thought —"

"Time enough to talk later, Liz. Right now we have to get to the president's palace. Your friend Tate Gilmore is going to assassinate the President."

"What? But why?"

Over his shoulder Father Miguel said, "He thinks he is saving your life."

When Carlos Valdez returned to the place where Liz Archer had been held he found two unconscious men. A hurried search of the place told him that Liz was gone.

He turned and ran out, hurrying to the president's palace.

Gilmore fired one shot . . .

"Abra la puerta," Soto commanded the Juaristas.

They pushed the doors open and rushed in with their rifles poised. Soto walked in behind them, then stopped short as he saw Juarez standing behind the desk.

"What —"

Off to one side stood Tate Gilmore, his gun in his hand.

"Soto," Juarez said. "I thought you had something to attend to?"

"I, uh, I did —"

Gilmore had only to look at the panic in the man's face to know that Soto was the inside man for the rebels.

"And you did say you were leaving one man in the hall?" Juarez asked.

"I, uh, decided to leave more —"

"Why? Did you feel that I was threatened by Señor Gilmore's presence?"

"I felt there was a possibility, Excellency."

"Then why did you leave me alone with him?"

Soto had no immediate answer.

Gilmore was watching the Juaristas carefully, not knowing where their loyalties lay.

"Eduardo . . ." Juarez said. "You want me dead, don't you? Did you think that if I was dead you would be president? Did you really believe that?"

"Excellency —"

"Arrest him!" Juarez ordered the Juaristas.

Gilmore still watched carefully to see what the men would do. Without hesitation they turned towards Soto, ready to obey their president. Soto had not included them in his plan. He simply had them standing by so that when Gilmore killed Juarez, they would in turn kill Gilmore.

Soto turned his body slightly to the left, his shoulders sagging, and then suddenly he turned towards Juarez, flashing a small derringer in his hand. The Juaristas were caught completely by surprise, but Gilmore quickly raised his gun and fired.

The bullet struck Soto in the forehead, jerking his head back violently and knocking him to the ground. Any other sort of shot might have left him time to pull the trigger and kill his president.

Juarez walked around the desk to where Soto lay, regarded the body solemnly, and then suddenly kicked Soto in the head.

"Remove him!" he told the Juaristas.

As the four men removed the body he said to Gilmore, "I owe you much."

"You don't owe me anything, Mr. President."

"Have another drink."

"I can't. I must try to save my friend now that I have not done what the rebels asked."

"I will send my men with you."

"That's not necessary. Their presence might spook the men I seek. I'll do it alone."

"Very well, but please come back to see me with your friend, before you leave Mexico City."

"I will, Excellency."

Gilmore left the office and hurriedly retraced the steps that had brought him there. He was anxious to find out if Father Miguel had carried out his part of the plan they'd hatched together the night before.

As Father Miguel and Liz reached the president's palace they stopped.

"How do we get in?" Liz asked, noting the guards at the fortress-like door.

"I might be able to simply walk in," Father Miguel said, "but I don't know about you."

"Then go ahead, Father. You've got to stop Tate before he —"

"Look!" Father Miguel said.

She looked up to see Tate Gilmore coming out the front doors and starting down the steps.

"Tate!" she shouted. Liz started to run up the steps but Father Miguel cautioned her.

"No quick moves or you will attract the guards."

"Tate!" she called again, and started up the steps to meet him.

"Liz!" she heard him reply.

They met halfway on the steps and stopped short, staring at each other. To her he looked terribly gaunt, as if he had lost a lot of weight. Whether that was because she had not seen him in a long time or as a result of his shooting, she didn't know. Other than his thinness, however, he looked fine.

"You look awful," she said.

"Thanks, you look wonderful."

"Thanks. What happened in there?"

He turned and looked up at the palace, and then back at her.

"The rebels are going to have to find themselves another inside man." He moved down one step and put his arm around her.

"Where've you been?"

"It's a long story," she said.

"Well," he said, tightening his arm around her, "we have a lot of time."

CHAPTER THIRTY-TWO

They spent the night together — not at the House of the Angels, but at Liz's hotel — where they compared notes on what had happened to both of them on their ways to, and once they arrived at, Mexico City.

They finally got around to Carlos.

"He is the rebel leader — or one of the rebel leaders," Liz told Tate. "He told me he'd help me find you, and the man who shot you. Now I know that he was trying to keep us apart until they decided how to use us. He was a good liar . . ."

"That may be, but I don't think his heart was very really in it," Gilmore said. "I think you got to him, Liz."

"I guess . . ."

"He could have turned over the man who shot me, you know. At any time."

"Really? How do you know?"

"Fuentes told me who the shooter was."

"Fuentes?"

"Yes . . . before he died."

Liz didn't miss the implication, but let it go.

"Who shot you, Tate?"

"Carlos Valdez."

The next morning over breakfast Gilmore told Liz that Juarez wanted to see them before they left Mexico City.

"Do you think he wants to offer us jobs as his bodyguards?"

"That might very well be," Gilmore said.

"What are you going to do now, Tate?"

"I've got to find Carlos ."

"You may have to fight your way through Mexican rebels to do that."

"Yes, I might . . . "

"You should rest. You're not fully recovered from your wound."

"That may be, but I won't ever be fully recovered until I find Carlos and settle with him."

"Well, if you insist on staying, then I'll stay, too."

"You don't have to —"

"There is a lot for us to talk about that we didn't discuss last night, Tate. When this is over I want to be around to do that."

"All right, then," he said, pushing away his coffee cup. "Let's go and talk to Father Miguel. He might be willing to help us."

"I doubt it," Liz said. "He may not have agreed with what Carlos and Soto were trying to do, but still he sympathizes with the rebel cause."

"There's no harm in asking."

"Tate, why would Carlos shoot you in the back, and then try to use you here in Mexico?"

"I was trying to break up the robbery he and his compadres were pulling and he wanted to stop me. My guess would be that when he heard I was on my way here he saw a way to use me before he had me killed. You just happened to get in the way because you wanted to help me, Liz."

"And so he decided to use me, too."

"Yes. Again, my guess is that either one — or both — of us would have done for their plans."

They stood up to leave and the waiter hurried over with their bill.

"Let me buy you breakfast," Liz said.

Although Gilmore's hand was in his pocket, he smiled and said "All right."

"I'll meet you outside."

Gilmore went outside while Liz gave the waiter some money and waited for her change. When she received it she went outside to meet him.

She did not see Gilmore immediately, but when she turned her head to the left she saw him down the street, looking in the window of a gun shop. She started walking toward him and glanced across the street.

At that moment she saw Carlos Valdez pointing a gun at Tate Gilmore. He was going to shoot him in the back.

Again!

She started running, her hand reaching for her gun, and she shouted, "Tate! Look out!"

Her shout attracted not only Gilmore's attention, but that of Carlos Valdez, as well. She fired once at Valdez, but he was tucked into a doorway and she could not hit him. The Mexican pointed his gun at Gilmore again, who was turning towards Liz.

"Tate!" she shouted again. She threw herself in front of him and he caught her with one arm while drawing his gun with the other. The force of her weight turned them around so that Gilmore was looking over her at Valdez.

Valdez fired and Gilmore fired a split second later. His angle was better than Liz's had been, and his bullet hit home, striking Valdez square in the chest. The Mexican staggered for a few steps and fell backwards through a shop window.

"It's all right, Liz," he said, "I got him."

He put his gun away and realized suddenly that he was supporting her entire weight with his arm.

"Liz?"

He held her in both arms and looked down at her back. He saw there was blood and it was flowing at an alarming rate.

Valdez had shot Angel Eyes in the back!

"Jesus, Liz!" he cried out.

He pressed his hand against her wound, trying to stem the flow of blood as he lowered her gently to the ground.

"Someone get a doctor!" he shouted at the gathering crowd. "Get a doctor, for God's sake!"

"Tate?"

"Yes, honey, I'm here," he said. He grabbed the orange bandana from around her neck and tried to use it to stop the blood, or at least to slow it down. When he gave it to her so long ago, he never expected to be using it for this purpose.

"I've . . . never been shot before."

"I know, I know. You'll be fine."

"It hurts."

"It hurts like hell . . ." he agreed.

"Those things we have to talk about," she said, fighting the pain, "you know . . . what they are . . . don't you?"

"I know, my Angel Eyes," he said, "believe me, I know . . . and we'll talk about them, very soon."